Food for Marriage

KEN CARLTON

For Florence,
who put the olives in the martini,
stem glass always

Cooking is the art of preparing food by the aid of heat, for the nourishment of the human body.

—Mrs. Simon Kandar, The Way to a Man's Heart

The Settlement Cookbook Tested Recipes from the Milwaukee Public School Kitchens, Girls Trades and Technical High School, Authoritative Dietitians and Experienced Housewives Copyright 1948

Food
for
Marriage

Part One
Amuse Bouche

- 1 -
LUCY

There was nothing in the world a long taut stalk of irises could not cure. Lucy sat up in bed with a jolt and pulled the two bottom slats of the Venetian blind apart a smidgen. The fresh light of day splintered into the bedroom.

"Jesus, what time is it?" Lionel grunted, rising above the crumple of the comforter on his elbows.

"Seven," she said, recoiling from his breath. Once the smell of stale smoke and whisky had turned her on at that hour. It was hard to imagine now. She sat on the edge of the bed and pulled on her jeans and the Save Haiti t-shirt she had peeled off the night before. She didn't bother to put on a bra.

"Where are you going?"

"The market."

"At seven in the morning?"

Granted, it was a bit early. No reason she couldn't lie awake thrashing for another hour or two, turning over the same litany in her racing mind again and again. Even the meds weren't putting her under for more than a few hours these days unless she washed them down with a large glass of red and Guttman had strongly advised against that, even as he declined to raise her dose.

"It's the best time," she said, kissing Lionel on his forehead. He did still have a rakish look about him, she thought. His hair was too long, and the salt was clearly starting to overwhelm the pepper. He hadn't shaved in a week, a habit that had become ritual of late.

Lucy stepped into the bathroom and looked at herself. She hadn't been to the hairdresser in two months. The auburn streaks were starting to show signs of gray. She wondered if she wouldn't look sexy in a professorial way if she let it go all the way, allow her true nature to take its course. Her mother had been gray since Lucy was in tenth grade. She used to be embarrassed – all of her friends' moms looked like they had just walked out of an ad for a Sandals Resort. She wondered what Isaac would think if he returned home from school and found his mother looking more like Emmylou Harris than Katie Couric.

"What market?" Lionel called out from bed. Usually he had fallen back asleep by now. She wondered what change in his unpredictable climatology was prompting this interest in her early morning activities. She pulled her hair back in a ponytail and curled a rubber band into it. There. That was more like it. AARP could wait. Maybe she'd get her streaks done later today.

"Union Square," she mumbled with a mouthful of toothpaste. She spit into the sink and admired herself for a moment. Not bad. She strolled back into the darkened bedroom.

"Luce?"

"Honey?" She sat down on the rumpled bedclothes beside her husband. He reached around her with one hairy

12

arm and pulled her close.

"You smell good."

"I do?"

"Mmmmm." He burrowed his head into her side and she felt his hand reach beneath her shirt. He cupped her breast, not sexually, but with the ardor of a little boy seeking comfort. At first.

"Hullo!" Lucy chirped. Amazing. All these years and he still knew precisely how to hit the right spot. "Someone seems to be waking up."

"Mmmm," he grunted again. "Sure you need to go?"

"We have six people coming for dinner tonight. You do remember, don't you?"

"Oh, that." The news didn't seem to distract him from his mission. She squirmed. Lionel had great hands. Pianist fingers. Adept in many ways. "We could order in pizza," he mumbled. The manicured nail on his long forefinger was making a compelling argument for a minor detour in her morning plans.

"You could save that thought," she said, gently removing the offending digit from her breast. She turned around on the bed and kneeled over him. She stroked his scratchy beard, and ignoring the scent of his breath, kissed him on the mouth. "I'll see you later."

Lucy double-locked the front door, stashed her keys in her pocket, walked down the carpeted hallway and summoned the elevator.

"Morning Mrs. Kaminsky."

"Hi Gus."

"You're up early," he said, sliding the caged door shut.

Why is everyone so interested in my sleep habits, she thought to herself. A dozen years in their tony address and she still sometimes felt like a stranger in their building. How many New Yorkers even knew there were still elevator operators employed in the city, much less coexisting on a first name basis with a staff full of them. She smiled ruefully to herself. It wasn't as if anyone held a gun to her head when she and Lionel had lucked into their Upper East Side junior six. Timing was everything, right? She bounded out into the mirrored and marble lobby.

"Morning Mrs. K."

"Hi Roberto," she said, greeting the weekend doorman.

"You're up early."

Good lord! Didn't anyone have anything better to contribute to the universal dialogue?

"Yes. Supposed to be a gorgeous day." She opted for the morning forecast ritual. That had served mankind well for passing chitchat over the last thousand years or so. Or at least since the advent of the doorman, who in Roberto's case was more than deserving of a cheerful salutation.

"You betcha, Mrs. K. Have a good one."

She bounced out the front door, drinking in the fresh air. She was, in fact, a morning person, which proved to be a boon in her new role as empty nester. Ever since Isaac had left for Cornell, her sleep habits had gone from poor to dismal. It was as if with the passing of a morning routine – even the grunt of her teenage son shuffling off to school had sufficed for something – now, her daily radar screen was disturbingly empty. The vacuum Isaac's departure created left her restless and uneasy. While she managed to wrestle with the newfound challenge of staying busy by day, the few dark hours of sleep at night were more problematic. It was as if her mind was searching for a conduit, and with none to latch onto, she sprung up endlessly throughout the night until daybreak at last released her. A dinner party was just the answer. She took a deep breath and set off for the subway.

It was a real *9/11* morning. She always felt that way when Labor Day passed and the calendar turned the page to crisp fall breezes and shocking blue skies. Even nine years hence, she could not help but think about it. More a glancing remembrance than anything else. She walked down 79th Street, which was all but devoid of humanity. An older man in worn slippers and a Burberry raincoat stood by a tree as his poodle watered the bushes. She guessed he was on a mission for a sleeping wife. She preferred not to think about what he might, or might not have on, beneath his trench coat. She turned right down Lex, where the foot traffic picked up.

How placid their neighborhood was. Lucy 2.0 – the grad school pre-Lionel version – could never have imagined herself in this rarified zip code. Then again, there were loads of things about her life Lucy never could have imagined. The list had offset her shrink's mortgage payment on his Bridgehampton place for the better part of a decade.

As she approached the hulking mass of Lenox Hill Hospital, a young Caribbean woman pushing a wheelchair asked her for the time. Lucy obliged. The young woman's charge was an elderly woman, her hair crisp and white.

"Thank you, young lady," the old woman said. And then added, "I get my hair done every Saturday by Francois at nine a.m."

"And that," Lucy replied, "is why you look so beautiful."

The caretaker and the old woman continued on their way. For a moment Lucy felt a deep tinge of guilt. She could swing by and visit her mother, but—. No! She was not going to let anything curb her enthusiasm this morning. God, what had inspired them to ever buy up here anyway? She navigated her way past two doctors immersed in conversation at the top of the 77th Street stairwell and plunged down into the dank yellow air of the Lexington Avenue subway station.

Sixty blocks south, she exited into the brilliant sunshine of Union Square. The Greenmarket was bustling like a county fair. So this was where they kept the heart and soul of New York. She felt a smile spread across her face. The crowded plaza was pulsing with energy. The crack of skateboards slapped off the pavement as a half-dozen unkempt boys preened like acrobats on wheels. Not a one of them could have been more than twelve. City kids. How she loved it down here. She wandered into the sea of stalls.

The market was a veritable orgy of produce. She zigzagged from stand to stand, drinking in the scent of fresh cilantro and sage and shrubby bunches of basil stacked six deep atop the tables. Bin after bin of apples – Romes and Winesaps and Macouns – beckoned. The sizzle of turkey scrapple caught her ear at the same time as the sweet spicy smell hit her. She stabbed a piece with a toothpick, offering a sheepish grin to the rough-hewn turkey guy from Di Paolo's as he laid out more samples from his well-worn Coleman stove. Did everyone feel as guilty as she did, she wondered, as the delicious burnt turkey flavor mingled with her coffee breath? Who bought ground turkey at eight in the morning anyway? She shrugged and moved on.

She came to a stop at the maze of crates and baskets at McDonough's Fresh Produce from Antrim, NY. The hand-lettered sign was scrawled on a weathered piece of barnboard. Lucy edged her way through the crowd, three deep even at this hour, until she made her way to the baskets bursting with potatoes. Yukon golds, Russian miniatures, fingerlings, Finna reds, rare French organic purples. Bliss! She could barely contain herself. Lucy liked to design her menu by sight, rarely making a list and hardly ever knowing what concoction might entice her on any given day. She was as eclectic as Picasso and the evening meal could turn out to be line-caught tuna that had been thrashing off the waters of Montauk a few hours ago, or a vegetarian lasagna simmered with the glorious, misshapen heirloom tomatoes that filled the market as far as the eye could see.

The dusty rows of hand-picked potatoes spoke to her. Even as she fingered through them, she was choreographing in her mind. Dinner for eight, and not just their usual stodgy group of occasional Upper East Side acquaintances. Tonight was for Nicole.

A brief email from her absolute best friend on the planet had prompted Lucy to round up the usual suspects. Dan, her stalwart university male friend and soulmate, and his wife Nora from the Upper West Side. Paula, with whom she shared her first Manhattan apartment only a thousand lifetimes ago, and her husband Chuck. They were hauling in from – horrors – New Jersey, where they were mired in raising their brood. And the cause celebre – Nicole's new "partner," Gray. What kind of name was Gray, anyway? She could almost hear the ivy accent emanating from a man with a large blocky head and very square shoulders in a tweed coat. Oh well, she'd know soon enough. Nicole had resurfaced and Lucy was having a party. She rubbed her hands with glee and decided potatoes were on the menu.

"I can take you, ma'am." The young farmer relieved her of plastic bag after bag of miniature gourmet spuds. He dropped each package on a dusty scale, tapping out a number on an old-fashioned adding machine. Lucy didn't even know where they got their electricity from, plunked down here in the middle of the street. The vendor had his long hair tied back and stashed in a bicycle cap sitting atop his head. His eyes were piercing and blue, clear as a stream with unbridled youth. Antrim was upstate, wasn't it? Maybe near Cornell. She wondered if Isaac had a muffin and his morning coffee wherever this gorgeous creature hung out. Funny, she could not get her son out of her mind. She and Lionel had dropped their precious one and only off for freshman orientation just a few weeks ago. Lucy's eyes pooled at the thought of it, the silence of the empty back seat, the vacuous still of their too-large car as they wended their way south back to the city. Lionel drove stone-faced, hands clutched to the wheel, his emotions a mystery, even as *she* blew her nose for the first fifty miles on the long drive home. She wondered if Isaac missed them at all.

"That'll be eighteen twenty-five."

"Can you break a hundred?"

He reached into his apron pocket and pulled out a thick wad of bills. Commerce on the fly. She loaded the potatoes into her Whole Foods burlap sack and moved on. What to make with the potatoes, she wondered, surveying the stalls. And then it hit her. A roast! Filet mignon. Simple. Perfect. And just one dish. She'd cook it at low heat in her oversized Williams-Sonoma roasting pan – the one she only brought out for Thanksgiving. Oil and salt the potatoes, place the tenderloin in a rack above them, and voilà. In the oven and out. That would free her up for the evening ahead. She did not want to be handcuffed to the kitchen. Not with her best friends coming.

Lucy tucked up to a stand jammed to its limits with local greens. A salad would certainly be in order, right? She gathered up bunches of lettuce – butterhead and romaine and bibb – and then some arugula and frisee and, oh my, fresh brussel sprouts. She stopped to admire the long gnarly sinuous green stalks. Risky choice. A lot of bad childhood memories tied into that one. Then again, what didn't taste delectable if you loaded enough butter and garlic and salt on board? Brussel sprouts it was. She'd do a quick last-minute stir fry while the roast was settling. She could picture Chuck's face, hauling back to the distant suburbs of New Jersey with Paula, complaining all the way home. *What the hell was the deal with the brussel sprouts?* Lucy didn't care. So Chuck could be a bit pedestrian. That was Paula's cross to bear.

With her sack filled, Lucy started to navigate her way out of the market. The crowd was growing thicker. How young down here, New York, she marveled. It was like the nuclear core for the entire city, all these kids in their 20s – they hardly seemed old enough to have jobs – handsome men, unshaven and scruffy, being dragged by fresh-faced girls in ponytails and baseball hats, Starbucks in hand, ears pierced two, three, four times. Their faces were riper than the groaning fruit stands. Lucy smiled at the whiff of nostalgia, drinking it all in as the day grew warm. Had she ever even been to the Greenmarket with Lionel? Doubtful. Maybe when she got home his surprising, buoyant mood would still be intact. When was the last time they made love in the morning? Better not to go there, she decided.

The subway entrance loomed up out of the crowd. She started down the stairs, and then stopped in her tracks. She had completely forgotten about her original mission. She reversed course, dodging a handful of people as she fought her way back up to the street. At the far end of the market she nudged her way into a flower vendor's stand and hastily grabbed three fresh bunches of iris. She forked over a twenty-dollar bill and tucked the flowers into her sack. Enough. It was a good start.

A few moments later she sat swaying on the hard orange bench seat of the Number 6 Train as it pulled into her stop at 77th Street. She looked at her wristwatch. It wasn't even ten a.m. She had hours until guests. Too many hours. She paused. The doors of the subway car opened. She had not been uptown in over a week. Nothing good could come out of a visit today. Not now, not with a houseful of people coming. And yet suddenly, the pull was gravitational. She took a deep breath, clenching her eyes and clutching her sack of produce as the doors sucked closed again. The train lurched out of the station.

She came out of the subway at Lenox Avenue and 116th Street. This was foolish. She checked behind her out of rote as she walked at a brisk clip, north. The renovated glassy highrises of the new Harlem clashed mightily with the bodegas and tenements and gutted-out lots. One moment, a rare flash of gentrified privilege, the next, a blueprint as desolate as a '70s snapshot. She had been up here enough times that she was no longer self-conscious about the color of her skin. She was only aware when others took note. Her Prada bag clashed with the filthy plastic Shoprite sacks that filled the shopping cart of a homeless man pushing a mountain of beer cans. The smell of stale urine was overpowering. The breeze was coming off the river. The vagabond's stench was still carrying a block away. She hoped it didn't cling to her clothes.

She turned right on 120th Street. Her pace quickened as Marcus Garvey Park loomed mossy and green to her left. At the corner of the park where it met Madison Avenue, she found her usual bench, just inside the perimeter. A lone dreadlocked man of perhaps thirty, with a powerful physique and mirrored glasses, tapped away at his BlackBerry. Lucy took a seat on the opposite side of the bench. The man did not look up. She crossed her legs and splayed her arms over the birdshit-stained slats. The sun cast grid-like shadows along the asphalt. She sat back and stared out of the park and across the street.

1901 Madison Avenue. The aging tenement building had seen some renovation over the years during one of Harlem's intermittent resurgences. Its limestone walls had met the abrasive wash of an owner's redo; the fire escapes had been painted at least in the last half-century.

From her perch, she could survey people as they came and went from the old apartment house. The double front doors were heavy and wooden, with scratched glass for windows, and nothing visible in the way of a lock that offered security. That came from within, where a dilapidated buzzer system was adhered to the wall, pocked with black button-like dots next to brass apartment numbers. Lucy knew them well.

She settled in. She did not have a lot of time today. The jubilant sound of youthful voices rose from the open doors of the Bethel Gospel Church, which sat caddy-corner to her post. A smile crossed her face. Three young black men strutted past, pausing to gawk at her. *Crazy white woman.* It was nice to be noticed.

She smiled back. A mother with a twin stroller rolled by, adjusting a blanket over a sleeping baby in the front seat. The back was loaded to the brim with groceries. A diaper bag hung from the handle. Lucy watched as the young woman continued on. Then she retrained her gaze on the entrance of 1901 Madison. The harmonies of the church chorus filtered high and carried into the thick grove behind her, summer clinging to its last gasp.

- 2 -
CHUCK

"Dad, are you coming?"

Jesus fucking Christ, Chuck muttered, yanking the sheets up over himself, his erection crumpling in his hand like a shrunken gerbil. So much for five concentrated minutes, eyes clenched tight, focusing every last ounce of his powers of imagination on his next-door neighbor's wife, who enjoyed washing her Volkswagen convertible in cutoff jeans and a tank top; the librarian-esque new bank loan officer he had met the other day; and a hasty last-minute homage to Nell Monahan, a college fling from a long-ago Rutgers Homecoming weekend. Good ol' reliable Nell had been on the verge of delivering him to the promised land when his daughter pushed open the partially ajar bedroom door. Was there no privacy? Mission not accomplished.

"Anyone ever hear of knocking around here?" Chuck asked, praying that his innocent, untarnished, nubile 17-year-old Melissa was spared the sight of her Dad frantically masturbating on a Saturday morning.

"Mom says get your ass out of bed."

"Nice mouth, Missy." Kids today.

"She said NOW."

"*She*, is your mother. Now if you can kindly get your ass

out of my room and give me two minutes, I'll be right down."
Chuck stared his daughter out the door, which she of course
left wide open. Oh well, he sighed. The mood was gone
anyway. He limped into the bathroom, wondering if there
was time to steal a quick shower.

"Planning to sleep all day?" Paula asked, rinsing a cereal bowl
as Chuck strolled into the kitchen a few moments later.

"Good morning to you too, honey. Any coffee left?"

"A drop. Some of us have been up for hours."

"Some of us would kill for an extra hour's sleep just
once in their life," he replied, hoping she bought it. Paula
loaded the rest of the breakfast dishes into the dishwasher as
she poured the remains of the coffee in a mug. She kissed
him on the cheek, even as she played her tiny sympathy violin
with her thumb and forefinger. It wasn't as if he couldn't
sleep eighteen hours a day if he chose. *Since.* She jammed the
thought out of her mind. The back door slammed open.

"Hey Mr. D., Mrs. D." Melissa's best friend Cyndi
Taylor strode in, followed by another stunning example of
teenage perfection who Chuck thought might be Carla Rose,
now unnervingly all grown up.

"Your Mom gave you her car?" Melissa squealed.

"All day," Cyndi said. "She and my Dad are going to
some stupid seminar in Philadelphia."

"That is so cool. Gotta go Mom," Melissa announced.

"Whoa, wait a sec," Chuck interrupted. "Honey," he said
turning to his wife. "Did we say anything about letting all
three girls drive to this thing?"

The "thing" was the New Jersey State High School
Cheerleading Championship tryouts. While Melissa and her
coterie were not members of the squad, they had to support
their friends and fellow classmates. So Missy had exhorted

Chuck and Paula the night before. Last Chuck recalled, the issue had remained unresolved.

"Missy, did I say you guys could drive?" Paula asked.

"Mom!" she protested, adding the requisite seven syllables to the title. "Cyndi's had her license for seven months. She's cool."

"By cool, I assume you mean legal?" Chuck inquired. There were more bylaws involving teenage driving than anything Chuck could begin to remember from his day. When he had learned to drive, he had tooled around the mall parking lot for a few weekends while his father read the business pages in the passenger seat – occasionally looking up to make sure Chuck wasn't pulling doughnuts at forty per. Then a three-page written test, a few minutes behind the wheel with a bored cop looking on, and that was that. Good to go in the eyes of the state of New Jersey. Chuck could have set off to Alberta with a half dozen friends and a bale of marijuana in a conversion van. As long as the pot was well hidden, his parents could care less. All that had changed. Now every parent was versed in which of the neighborhood kids had cleared their provisional permit requirements and were legally allowed to shepherd bands of precious youth back and forth across the treacherous parkways and turnpikes of the Garden State. Every parent except Chuck, it seemed.

"Yes, Dad, Cyndi is cool," Missy dripped. Did they teach Sarcasm 101 at Summit High or was it just contagious like swine flu, Chuck wondered. When would the Daddy's Little Girl phase kick in? This teen stuff was hell. Though Carla Rose in a V-necked t-shirt and obscenely thin white cotton shorts certainly smoothed things over.

"At least we don't have to carpool," Paula said, whacking Chuck out of an inappropriate fantasy that threatened to send him scurrying back upstairs to the bedroom on some imagined chore. Surely there was laundry to be folded.

"And we have to head into the city by five, anyway," she added. "Lucy said be there at seven. By the time we park and all."

"Do we really have to go?"

Paula shot him the hairy eyeball. That verdict had been handed down weeks ago. It wasn't that he minded Paula's best friend. Lord knows Lucy could whip up a scary good meal, and Lionel packed a mean bar with the finest hooch. But dare he admit he was running out of new material? Nine months of unemployment with no end in sight had left him a bit of a stuttering social misfit. He wasn't sure he had the stomach to be cheerful and entertaining tonight. Apparently that reality had not entered his wife's thinking.

"Bye Daddy." Melissa surprised him with a kiss on his unshaven cheek.

"Have fun, peanut. Love you." He watched as the three girls bounded out the back door, giggling all the way to the car.

- 3 -
DAN

Is that him? Dan wondered, picking up his pace jogging through the Park. He always felt his strongest during his runs when he hit the flattened out Park Loop at the Museum Mile on the East Side. How he longed for a Kevin Bacon sighting. Just a fleeting intersection – his shining moment to be one of the six degrees of separation.

Of course everyone knew that Kevin lived on the Upper West Side, along with his wife Kyra and their two children. But that didn't mean it might not be him out for a walk on the east side of the Park, along with thousands of others, meandering about on a beautiful early autumn afternoon. What dyed-in-the-wool New Yorker hadn't experienced a Kevin Bacon sighting? One need merely live in the vicinity of Broadway in the Eighties and make it a habit of grabbing their *Daily News* at the subway kiosk at 79th Street, or wander through the 84th Street Barnes and Noble, or be so lucky as to happen upon him at Barney Greengrass grabbing a fresh, softball-sized onion bagel smeared with a generous dollop of mouthwatering whitefish salad. The city reduced all its denizens to the most mundane of routines, rock star to street urchin. It did not play favorites. It was why Dan loved it so. There were other higher octane celebrities to be had. Dustin, for example. Spike. Alec. Dan had run into Pacino so often that they were nearly on a first name basis. At least in his mind.

But he had special designs on Kevin Bacon because Dan, in his younger days, was often compared to the ruddy thespian who had so imprinted himself on the acting community's consciousness in *Diner* and *Footloose* and *A Few Good Men.* Dan's agent, not a mere two months ago, had forwarded along a rejection note from a top casting director who had actually written in response to Dan's work. *We were on the fence with Dan Peterson. He brought a Kevin Bacon-like intensity to the screen test, but in the end the director was looking to skew a bit younger than your client played. Please feel free to submit him again any time.* True, you could grow hair in your ears waiting for that kind of break, but still, Dan persevered.

He picked up his pace, glancing backwards to assess his Bacon prey, who, naturally, turned out not to be Kevin Bacon. Not even a resemblance upon further examination. Dan thumped on.

What would he have done were it the man himself? In pursuit of his acting breakthrough, Dan had stooped so low that he had not only quit his latest dead-end job as a stage manager for an events company, but he'd even engaged in the ingratiating exercise of scripting his own one-man show. The hook of his magnus opus was that he played it from the pulpit of an indie rock star. A rock star who resembled Kevin Bacon, who happened to – in real life – comprise one half of the popular rock band The Bacon Brothers. Dan had gone to see them play in a swill and sawdust dive in Williamsburg and was so inspired by Kevin's hipster musical persona that he had gone back to the well and done a page-one rewrite of his show to feature his new Brooklyn Bohemian voice, since that had firmly entrenched itself as the flavor of the month in the best casting circles.

Manhattan had fallen out of favor for starving creative types. After all the years Dan and Nora had struggled to support their fifth floor walkup on Amsterdam Avenue, now it was de rigueur to be living in a Red Hook loft with six roommates over a rivet factory turned artist space and fair trade coffee shop. Where in hell was Red Hook anyway? Somewhere out by Ikea as best Dan could tell. But after a few hours of online research and an afternoon buried in countless issues of *New York* magazine, he became fluent in Brooklyn hipster. Anything to get that next audition – short of bumping into Kevin himself and begging him to take a look at his script. Degrading for sure, but Dan had heard plenty of far more humiliating stories that had led to an actor's first break. Overnight success was a long time coming. A kidney transplant might have been an easier score.

Dappled sunlight splashed through the trees as he kicked into high gear at 86ᵗʰ Street. Couples lolled on blankets spread out across the grass tumbling down to the slanted mirror-blue windows of the Metropolitan Museum of Art. The road hooked right and then left as Dan whizzed by the curated palaces on Fifth: Cooper-Hewitt, The Jewish Museum, The Museum of the City of New York. This was Lucy country, he thought, his Nikes springing off the pavement as he left the walkers and tourists behind. The *clack slap clack* of an online skater made him turn his head. Those guys could kill you they carved such a wide swath.

What kind of wine did I say I'd bring? He could not remember for the life of him. Oh well. It wasn't like Lucy and Lionel needed his meager contribution. Even if he splurged and scored a twenty-dollar bottle, he knew they'd thank him and then relegate it to the maids who'd be steam-cleaning the apartment the next morning.

Despite a relationship dating back to Dan and Lucy's Brown days, he still had trouble imagining his liberal, activist, pot-smoking friend, who used to wait tables at a Providence vegan restaurant, now ensconced in her spacious Upper East Side apartment. No one was more understated about her wedded wealth than Lucy, and Dan had carte blanche to tease her mercilessly about it. All the same, he never set foot in her place unless Lucy rolled it out for one of her beloved foodie shindigs. Theirs was more a friendship of coffee shop eggs and East Village dive bars. Dan wasn't sure if Lionel could find McSorley's with a map. Just as well. Lionel was the side dish for the evening, salty like fries and filling in a pinch. Lucy was the main course. She was why they came.

A few moments later, Dan hiked up the five flights of stairs to his apartment. He plucked the key from his running shorts pocket and let himself in.

"I'm home," he announced, drenched from his exercise.

"You stink," Nora said, not even looking up, her back to him in front of the computer.

"Watcha doing, love?" he asked, nuzzling her neck from behind all the same.

"Just a little work," she replied, flexing her shoulders to cover the screen. Dan wrapped his sweaty arms around her and peeked in, but the images had already faded to screensaver. "How was your run, sweetheart?" Nora asked, pushing him away from the monitor.

- 4 -
WHERE LUCY GOT
HER GROOVE ON

There was something insane about shopping at Lobels. On the other hand, Lucy thought, there was also something tantalizing – almost sexual about it. All those men handling thick, obscene red cuts of meat, servicing a clientele comprised of predominantly attractive, well-heeled women, in sharp contrast to the shabby Harlem park bench where she had finally torn herself away. The toned thighs in spandex nearly outnumbered the firm marbled cuts of Porterhouse and New York Strip lining the glass case at the front of the Upper East Side meat emporium. This was serious business and Lucy had lofty intentions for the evening's do. It was not every day you met your best friend's new love. Not at their age. Not in Lucy's life. Nicole was the first of the nucleus club to bring a second model to the floor. This called for prime beef.

"Help you, ma'am?" Lucy smiled with vague recognition at the butcher in his pressed white apron. They must have had a team of laborers doing the real slaughterhouse stuff in the back, because the front guy's smock was so pristine that he looked like he had just walked out of a J. Crew ad, only for carnivores.

"Yes, please." Lucy pursed her lips, her facing forming a perfect oval, her bangs rounding out her unmade-up face. Ever since her potato epiphany at the Greenmarket, she'd been fantasizing about a filet mignon roast. But now the sight of a delicate rack of lamb in the case was throwing her all for a tizzy. Lamb for eight – and she could whip up a tangy mint and lemon sauce to paint the tasty red chops – would certainly be a showpiece. Then again, she was so eager to see Nicole, eager to see everyone, in fact, that the simplicity of the filet held its own appeal. Less time in the kitchen and more time to hang with her friends.

"Ma'am?" The butcher woke Lucy from her culinary daze. The woman behind her was tapping her iPhone against the palm of her hand impatiently.

"How about a whole tenderloin to feed eight?" Lucy decided.

"Okay. Four to five pounds should do the trick. Kobe, Wagyu or prime organic?"

"Mmmm." Decisions, decisions. Every bone in her body wanted to say Kobe but for the cost of the buttery, Japanese, grass-fed beef. If she followed her gut, they might have to take out a new mortgage. Lionel had been reprimanding her of late about unnecessary cash outlay. Times were tough and they needed to rope it in, he had said. She wondered if it was the tough times or her husband's cold streak that was driving their new economy. While they were plenty south of the one percent, it wasn't like they were suffering, and for this, her conscience suffered mightily. She also had to consider environmentally friendly, locavore Dan, for he would surely excoriate her if she went Kobe (even as he devoured it). *Do you have any idea what a dent you put in the carbon footprint just to get this roast all the way from Osaka?* She could already hear his tirade.

"Skip the Kobe," she informed the butcher. "Organic, please. Make it five pounds." Score one for Al Gore. Thank God she had Dan to remind her of her roots. Everything did not come so easily to her, despite appearances, trapped in her outwardly, infinitely comfortable life. No matter how many volunteer events she chaired, or how much money she and Lionel channeled into the right functions, the right charities, the right causes – she could not escape the lurking sense that somehow, somewhere she had made a wrong turn. There was a day she had envisioned herself following in the footsteps of Sandra Day O'Connor as the new feminine voice on the Supreme Court. Or at the very least, making her mark as the Democratic Senator from the great State of New York. Law school was the plan when she and Dan set forth from Providence. How bright and near a star in their unique galaxies it all seemed, Dan shipping off to Juilliard on a drama scholarship, even as she reveled in the news of her acceptance to University of Virginia School of Law.

Three years later, law degree all but in hand and a juicy selection of elite New York firms queued up and awaiting her services, Lucy sat rapt and watched as the young governor from Arkansas heralded change. "You have raised your voices in an unmistakable chorus. You have cast your votes in historic numbers. And you have changed the face of Congress, the Presidency and the political process itself. You, my fellow Americans, have forced the spring. Now we must do the work the season demands."

His inaugural address had made Lucy want to sow some wild oats. The bourbon-tinged accent, that lion's mane of hair, the palpable presence – the shivery charge that pulsed through her as he spoke. His words elicited tears as Lucy watched, and it inspired her to enlist. When notification of her White House internship arrived via an embossed envelope, her decision was a no-brainer. Wall Street could wait. She would plant the seeds of change with this powerful new figure.

A year later, Lucy's fate collided with political reality – literally! – as she ran through the hallowed halls of the West Wing, arms stacked with folders that, to this day, she could not recall what they were. Her head was down, heels clicking, as she raced to deliver her goods to the Assistant Deputy Secretary of Administrative Affairs, when she crashed full body into the leader of the free world.

Papers flew like leaves across the floor. Her face burned crimson as she sought the words to apologize for bowling over her boss. Where was the Secret Service? Where was the entourage, as she found herself, a lowly intern, on hands and knee with the President of the United States. It was not how she imagined her first rendezvous with power would be. No experience, no classes, could prepare her for diplomacy at this level.

His hair was sandy, his physical countenance more pronounced up close than she had imagined. As he helped her gather up a sheaf of reports, she noticed that his hands were large, his fingers long and tapered. She could feel the sweat beneath her arms, and prayed it was not showing through her silk blouse. At least a minute had gone by and no one had stumbled upon them. Their business done, he asked her name.

"Lucy Kaminsky," she said. "From New York." It sounded so, Jewish, she thought, and still he did not move. The two of them stood alone in the corridor and then, when there seemed nothing more to say – and to this day she still wondered, did he actually say it? – the words summoned from his lips: "Would you like to step into the Oval Office?"

Lives hinge on a moment. Careers launched, fortunes made and broken. In the roaring silence of her 25-year-old head, standing in a White House hallway, Lucy Kaminsky bridged that first crevasse. Because Lucy just said no.

- 5 -
NICOLE

Nicole did not just say no.

It was not for lack of trying. She had been to enough conferences and meetings in her life to recognize trouble when it came knocking. It was not the first time a colleague had eyeballed her in that certain way men did, especially when she put on some lipstick and pulled her hair back in a fashionable ponytail and wore a clingy silk blouse or form-fitting sweater. Men were so obvious. How often she and Lucy had marveled at their inelegant ways. Boys had not come far from throwing spitballs in fifth grade, they agreed – a mere step beyond cave men with a wooden club and an erection. But this time it was different. Randy Hawkins was not on the prowl. It was something else and she knew it the moment they met.

Had anyone asked Nicole five minutes before she rode down in an elevator with this handsome stranger – the two of them enroute to a mandatory business dinner of the most boring degree – that she would ever dream of straying from her appointed course, she would have scoffed in their face. Nicole was half Japanese by birth, though she had never met her birth father and genetically laid claim to only enough of her Japanese gene pool to boast a soupcon of the exotic good looks of a Geisha combined with the all-American verve of a UCLA cheerleader. As a result, her single years were not wanting in attention. Men clamored for her and she was not one to back down from experience. By the time she wed, Lucy was the only person in the world who knew half the interesting things Nicole had done, and they both agreed that some secrets were best kept that way. Ten years and two children later, in Nicole's mind it would have taken a seismic event to shake her from the heavily fortified pillars of her domestic foundation. So why was a chance encounter at a broadcasting conference – this non-threatening tete a tete – one iota different from the thousand that had preceded it? Because, she realized looking back, Randy Hawkins, minor media star in his own mind and not many others, made her laugh. So much so, that in the end, Nicole laughed herself right out of a marriage.

Her unsuspecting husband was beyond reproach and undeserving of what lay in wait beyond the three-tiered buttercream cake, their first dance, and the blissful twelve days in New Zealand, where she had dutifully sealed the deal. As scripts go, Nicole could not fault Bill. Even his name reeked of stability. William Tenner M.D. was a skilled surgeon with a gentle bedside manner and a successful Washington, D.C. practice. His prestige and standing were a mere complement to his flawless background. The guy was as pure and driven as the Cape Cod sand beneath their newly-wedded toes. He was a man destined for success and Nicole was the woman destined for him.

It was hard to deny that she was content at first. Nicole found work as an up-and-coming news producer at a local D.C. station. The home she and Bill purchased – a rundown nineteenth century brick Federal townhouse in Georgetown – was lovingly restored. They gave good parties with interesting friends and their sex life was perfectly adequate. When Nicole became pregnant with Justin, she thought that might smooth over her growing uneasiness. But not long after he was born, she found herself out of the workplace and home alone with a squawling infant. Her angst only seemed to grow. She was supposed to be dodging bombs in Somalia and taking home Peabody Awards – not hundred-count crates of diapers from the Super Giant.

The birth of Emily two years later was so sudden that Nicole sometimes wondered if her daughter's unplanned appearance wasn't merely a byproduct of a bad day of postpartum depression. A couple of martinis or a weekend down by the Delaware shore might have been a better solution. *C'est la guerre.*

Nicole trained herself to ignore the sense of malaise that followed her to bed every night. She played the role, drove the car pools, and showed up for the Christmas parties. She exercised her wifely duties with nary a complaint. Bill, a regimented lover and superb sleeper, apparently never noticed the tear-soaked pillow on his wife's side of the bed. A whispered schnuffle was not going to deter his eight hours.

It might have gone on like that indefinitely, because Nicole was loyal to a fault. That was, until Randy. It was he who convinced her, with his disarming smile and supreme confidence, that two people of the opposite sex could become intimate friends over emails and drinks, without crossing the line and upsetting the delicate balance of marriage. His marriage, hers – he seemed unconcerned with whose. And Nicole trusted him. Or at least she trusted herself. Right up until the moment when, with a healthy dose of doubt, fear and boarded up lust, her self control went right out the window, along with everything she had built over the course of thirteen years.

Wracked with guilt as thick and real as Beltway traffic, Nicole knew it wasn't Bill who unleashed this tempestuous landmine in their marriage. He might as well have been an innocent bystander to a fiery wreck. No one, least of all her adoring husband, could fathom that her outwardly fabulous life was steeped in an underlying current of rampant dishonesty. Had Bill known, he would have gotten her all the right help, assigned all the best doctors, and ensured that she was prescribed enough meds to lift the spirits of an elephant. Bill liked to fix things. But the one thing he could not repair was what Randy discovered laying dormant in Nicole for far too many years. She just did not do domestic well. That was her dirty little secret.

The irony, thought Nicole as she packed her overnight bag for her first visit to New York since the divorce, was that she had dismantled her life over an affair that didn't even last. Bill found out. Randy continued his marriage unscathed. But Nicole could not summon the strength to rebuild. Some damaged homes required renovation. Hers was in need of a teardown. The fact that her emotional architecture happened to plunder two innocent kids' childhoods was keeping a phalanx of psychiatry professionals employed. What she couldn't pave over with Xanax, she assuaged with the familiar words from Ecclesiastes, that her shrink had so generously provided.

A time to build up, a time to break down.
A time to dance, a time to mourn.
A time to cast away stones.
A time to gather stones together.

She serenaded Justin and Emily to sleep every evening to

the Byrds version of *Turn, Turn, Turn*, singing softly in the kaleidoscope glow of their spinning night-lights, willing the hurt away for all of them. That was, on the nights stipulated "her week" in the pages of the painstakingly crafted divorce agreement.

Her cell phone jingled. She recognized the number and picked up. "Hi," she said almost breathlessly.

"Sweetheart, are you ready?" The sound of Graydon's voice still sent a shiver of delight through her. She closed her eyes with satisfaction.

"I'll be there in fifteen minutes," she replied.

She slipped her phone in her purse. There'd be plenty of time to explain it all to Lucy, later. Time to round up the kids. Her overnight bag was packed. It was a short ride to Gray's. She wondered how much time they had before their train.

- 6 -
LIONEL

They had come again at dawn, the palpitations. He was barely a click past fifty – he couldn't be having a heart attack already, could he? It was not quite pain that had aroused him from sleep, just a pressure, a hint at his own mortality. He had rolled over in a cold sweat, clutching for Lucy as if in a dream. Where was she now? he wondered, listening to the silence of the apartment. Then he remembered. She had thrown on some clothes and headed out the door shortly after his latest myocardial scare. Something about shopping. Lionel glanced at the clock. Ten a.m. Half the morning gone. He sat up in bed, very much alive to face another day.

He stumbled into the kitchen in search of his morning fix. He washed down the Lipitor with a swill from a leftover Starbucks of unidentifiable vintage. Who cared. It did the trick, loosening the tightness in his chest, or so he imagined. In his mind, he visualized the oval-shaped, twenty-milligram pill dissolving in his bloodstream, working like tiny brushes to scrub his arteries clean and keep the blood pumping. Lord knows he needed it. He had been taking shitty care of himself of late. Slices for lunch. Stolen smokes on his long walks through Central Park. Last night he had wolfed down half a pound of raw chopped meat at two in the morning, mixed up with an egg yolk and some ungodly combination of salts from his private collection. Smoked pink from the Himalayas. Coarse Gris de Guarande, hand harvested from the marshes off the west coast of France. Anything that bit back, mixed in with a little Dijon mustard and a finely chopped shallot. *Steak Tartare de Lionel.* It was a bad habit he had picked up as a child, sampling the meat from his mother's mixing bowl when she made Shepherd's Pie for himself and his siblings, before she took off with his father on their regular Saturday night date. Other kids' moms left a greasy sack of fish and chips and mushy peas with the nanny. Not his mother. Miriam Birnbaum left square meals prepared for the babysitter with firm instructions for bedtime.

Raw meat and music. The two things his Mum had given him. On Sunday afternoons, when all the other boys in Kensington were glued to the football matches, Lionel's mother was dragging him to Royal Albert Hall: a mere child, not a half-dozen years old. They'd sit side by side, mother and son, watching the performances of the London Symphony Orchestra under Andre Previn. At first, Lionel had to be coaxed. But in time he came to love the exciting, jazzy style the young conductor brought to the stage. It was not dull, like the insufferable BBC broadcasts they listened to on weekend drives to visit his aunties. This was live and real and packed with emotion. He'd clutch his mother's hand as the tympani pounded and the horns blared and the violins played as one, all building to an inevitable crescendo as the tears welled up in his eyes. Obviously the experience stuck, he mused, dumping the curdling Starbucks down the sink. There was a time he even thought it had paid off.

Bright daylight streamed into the apartment as the sun rose above the towering buildings across the way on 79th Street. Lionel meandered into the bathroom and stared at his face in the mirror. He looked more exhausted than usual, like he was seeing his grandfather staring back at him with the bulging chicken-puffed eyelids. He needed that final wee dram last night like a hole in the head. As if it could somehow snap him out of his malaise, a blue period that was starting to feel like it might outlast the recession. Now he recalled. Nicole was coming tonight. They all were. A reunion of Lucy's childhood. Lionel sighed, sucking in his gut as he walked past the full-length mirror.

What had he done to get so lucky, he wondered, washing down an aspirin with the leftover scotch water in the Waterford crystal glass on his night table. Lucy deserved better. He lived in fear of her one day waking up to that blunt realization. He sat down on the edge of the bed heavily. Maybe the whisky dregs would provide a little hair of the dog comfort. That, or a few months at Betty Ford. Did anyone even still go there?

He pulled on a pair of well-worn corduroys and a loose-fitting button-down oxford. Writing clothes. Only the last thing in the world he felt like doing was writing. He wandered over to the corner of the bedroom and peered out the window across the street. An entire opposing edifice stared back at him, populated with people who actually had something to do on a glorious Saturday morning. Like his lovely wife for example, who had shot out the door at dawn, purportedly to the market. *Hmmm.* Her laptop, he noticed, was open on the Chippendale desk that served as her makeshift office. He wiggled the mouse toggle and her Gmail account opened. Maybe he should scan her inbox. Who knew what secrets might lie buried in its digital stash? With her trim, svelte body and jet-black hair, she was a direct counterpoint to his expanding waistline and weary visage. She had once said that his age – ten years her senior – was sexy.

That was back when he could find his abs, before he crossed the great divide into fifty.

How he ended up with such a stunning young woman like Lucy was no mystery. It was the music. Always the music. The year he was discovered, Lionel Birnbaum was an unheard-of virtuoso from Manchester. He had been conducting a ragtag symphony in a blue-collar city on a shoestring budget and a dream. Then, through a fluke of staggering proportions, he was invited to New York to guest conduct the majestic Philharmonic at Lincoln Center. It was a mere half season, three months filling in. He was a youngster in a dying business and his youth was as cherished as his talent. In the final week, he led Mahler's Fifth — and what a stunning performance it was. The orchestra he'd temporarily inherited was so skilled that a novice could have conducted it. And what more was he than a hopeful neophyte back then. When the final notes faded, he slowly turned around on stage in his starched shirt, sweat drenching his forehead, and stared out at the appreciative audience thundering its approval with a standing ovation. It was then that life played one of those small tricks that only artists and magicians can conjure.

There in the front row stood Lucy Kaminsky, a second-year associate in a first class law firm, occupying the premium seat of a partner who had taken ill at the last moment. Lucy, coming off a series of failed relationships with boys not men, had nothing better to do with her evening, so she had accepted the pair of tickets, knowing even then that she would not be able to find a taker for the companion seat. She graced Lionel's uninterrupted view of the house sheathed in a simple white dress, standing out in a sea of black chiffon. She applauded with a focused solemnity, her eyes piercing through the stage lights to meet his. Were Bernstein conducting, he would have cued the orchestra to strike the first notes of *Maria*, Lionel thought. This beautiful woman's gaze was so disconcertingly serious that he glanced around to see if it was the first violin she had ferreted out. But it was him. When he returned for his final bow, the gadabouts in the orchestra seats had begun to make their beeline to the exit. But Lucy stood erect, still clapping. He was unable to tear his eyes off of her. Just as it became apparent that he could not remain on the stage forever, she raised one hand, signaling with her perfectly manicured fingers and nodding toward the side door of the concert hall. "Five minutes," she lip-synched. Twenty years later he could still recall the moment as if it were yesterday.

The chest pains vanished by mid-morning. They always did. Ignoring them was Lionel's version of prophylactic care. He figured if his arteries were really as clogged as the Major Deegan at rush hour, the phantom palpitations would not disappear so readily.

He padded through the maze-like apartment looking for some more leftover coffee to reheat. The place felt too damned large and immaculate ever since Isaac left for college. He and Lucy had vacillated on the purchase years ago when the money had come in. Conducting, as glamorous as it seemed to the masses, had not gotten them much further than an Upper West Side walkup. Lionel had often amused cramped rooms full of friends, regaling them with the unfortunate economic realities for New York's performing coterie, many of whom had played under his baton. Illustrious as a seat in the Philharmonic might seem, the orchestra's finest musicians were more apt to be riding the B Train home to Brighton Beach at midnight with an oboe case tucked under their arm. There was no money in classical music, only glory. And glory did not pay the rent. Royalties did, which was why Lionel Birnbaum, when not guest conducting in Lima or Cleveland or Dubrovnik, wrote. His Symphony in G Minor had debuted at the Berlin Music Festival in the early 1990s. His Sonata for Three Cellos had gone on to become a minor hit for the Wagner label, back when selling 3,000 albums registered in *Billboard's* classical music charts. But in the end, it was the hastily scribbled ditty that vaulted him into the big leagues. A one-key melody so simple a child could hum it – and upwards of a hundred million probably did – when his most elegiac composition found its way to the title track of a silly and forgettable Broadway show. A show that became a blockbuster Hollywood movie that spawned a revenue stream that to this day still poured forth for Lionel and Lucy like a trusty old garden spigot that could not be turned off.

Lionel wandered into the corner room study, where his beloved Steinway Baby Grand sat. It was positioned so that he could sit on his bench and see all the way to the early morning mist rising from the East River. It was an inspiring view, one that had vexed him for years. Mahler composed. Previn composed. Bernstein composed. Lionel had been reduced to doodling. Try as he may, whenever he thought of Beethoven, all that came out was Disney.

He lifted the piano cover and opened his dog-eared composition book. He scrutinized the music before him, the squiggles and ink blotches an invisible language to all but himself. Would anyone notice or care if he ripped the book to shreds and flung it out the twelfth floor window? Sometimes he felt as if the future of classical music rested on his shoulders. What ten-year-old was going to choose an afternoon of chamber music at the 92nd Street Y over a bracing game of Xbox, or perhaps eight straight hours of YouTube? Were he not to complete his composition and make it sing to the gods, who would carry the torch? *Lionel's Unfinished Symphony.* A generation deprived. Click. Download. Share. Delete.

His long fingers pressed at the well-worn keyboard. The notes came slowly at first. He played the familiar refrain, almost in a whisper, like he did not trust his own craft. Then, hunched over, he reprised the notes with more urgency, until the chamber filled with sound. His eyes closed and his shoulders swayed as he played by rote the movement that had torn at him for months, seeking its conclusion. He let it take him away until the last note died. He lifted his fingers from the keyboard. The timbre still echoed through the room.

"It's stunning, honey."

"Ahhh," he yelped, startled.

Lucy wrapped her arms around his neck. He lolled his great head back into her soft breast, his unruly salt and pepper mop burrowing deeper into her. It had been a long night. He would have happily dug himself straight into Lucy's core and never climbed out again.

- 7 -
PAULA'S LAMENT

She pushed the vacuum cleaner with a fury that surprised her, like she had a vendetta against the old Electrolux, taunting her with its very age and resistance to breathe life into their tired wall-to-wall carpeting. The house had grown as empty as a church. Melissa and the girls had won their not very hard-fought battle to drive down to Trenton for the cheerleading competition. Chuck had skulked off to the gym in a last-ditch effort before their evening plans to squeeze in some semblance of exercise. For a man who had been home most every day for the past nine months, he had an enormous amount of difficulty getting anything done, Paula thought, steaming up and down the upstairs hallway. He acted like someone who had been sentenced to a prison term the day he was let go, only that would have been merciful because a prison term had limits, even parole for good behavior. Chuck's stay in unemployment Purgatory was becoming intolerable for everyone, its tentacles reaching far beyond his own bruised ego.

A coin sucked up into the vacuum cleaner with a clattering rattle. She hoped it wasn't a quarter and shut off the machine to find the perpetrator as it plunked back down to the carpet.

Jesus, had it become that desperate?

Chuck's layoff had been a complete shock. Bad news had leapfrogged from the newspapers and the Web and begun to spread with alarming frequency, even in their comfortable New Jersey suburb, forty-five minutes from Wall Street. The casualty count was growing, the at-home Dads popping up more and more, like unexpected dandelions in a September lawn. In the early stages they stayed camouflaged. Along with their generous packages, they were offered career counseling, skills seminars, and a carefully crafted menu of HR classes, which they gulped up like hungry goldfish. Any excuse to stay in town. No one wanted to be caught mowing the lawn in the middle of the workday. But all the cheery bells and whistles in the world could not change what was becoming evident: the jobs were not coming back.

Unfortunately for Paula, Chuck's golden parachute was devoid of the fat severance check and the six-month stay of execution. He had made his hay in software architecture, riding the wave until it crested and crashed back down to sea level. On the Friday evening of his last employed day, she had pasted on a sickly grin that felt as thin as generic vodka, even as she greeted him in a cheerful yellow sundress and a manufactured insouciance. She made a big deal of grilling an extra large hunk of wild Scottish salmon from Wegman's on their sleek, gas-fired Weber as they sipped icy margaritas on the back deck and donned a veil of blasé indifference.

"I can always go back to work," she said, fighting back the terror she felt at the mere prospect of a job interview after fifteen years in the suburban trenches.

"Don't be silly," he reassured her. "I have irons in the fire already. Besides, now I can finally get around to resurfacing the driveway." Paula laughed a little too loudly and planted an obvious kiss on Chuck's lips, as if newly blacktopped pavement was as much an aphrodisiac as a week in St. Barts.

Eight months later, the unwieldy black metal tubs of do-it-yourself sealant were still cluttering the garage, unopened. Apparently it was easier to tell her how to economize at the grocery store than to spread fifty gallons of black stinking goo on their cracked driveway with a stiff-bristled broom.

Up until the year of Chuck's demise, Paula had contentedly served as a member of the Summit High School PTA. She had begun as a volunteer on the athletic committee when Missy's older brother, Tommy, was a sophomore just starting out as a varsity basketball player. His eleventh grade growth spurt not only led him to an MVP season averaging seventeen points a game, but also had the effect of turning the entire family into athletic supporters. Tommy's senior year flew by in a blur of road trips and tournaments, and then college visits to Maryland, Ohio State, and Purdue. By the time Syracuse accepted him on a partial scholarship, the Dempsters had logged enough hours in the school gym and on the back roads of New Jersey to earn a spot in the parenting hall of fame. When Missy entered tenth grade, Paula was swayed to take on a bigger role with the PTA. Of course the friends who did the swaying had husbands as invested in Wall Street as the mothers were in bake sales. The two made for easy bedmates. With Tommy off to college, Paula had time on her hands, so she acquiesced. Chuck was raking it in and her new position proved to be busier than anything she had anticipated, filling her days with meaningful commitment, something she knew she'd been lacking for too many years.

Paula had never intended to drop permanently out of the workforce. She and Chuck were newly married and comfortably ensconced in their budding careers and a Murray

Hill one bedroom with a killer view and a full service gym. Family planning was not on their youthful agenda, but neither was her inadvertent pregnancy and the birth of Tommy. After her paltry maternity leave had expired, she gallantly soldiered on, fueled by the prospect of inflated bonuses being handed out like candy at the financial services firm where she worked. Armed with her Coach bag and a wheezy breast pump, she got through the worst of it and her star was once again on the rise. A nanny was employed and the apartment filled with the flotsam and jetsam of New York babyhood. Life was recasting itself as normal. Then Missy came along. Game, set, match.

Like the settlers before them, Paula and Chuck crossed the Hudson. Chuck was clearing six figures, they had two under two, and their new home needed things. Like furniture, for example. Paula didn't even pretend she was returning to the firm. Before she knew it, *The Wall Street Journal* became as extraneous to her as the Magna Carta and in what seemed like the blink of an eye, her worldview was formed by minivans, Costco, and the newfound language of New Jersey moms. It's only temporary, Paula told herself, as the pre-school years flashed by like road markers. Doubt followed her like a shadow as she watched her best friends soar to the expected heights. Had anyone suggested fifteen years ago that her net contribution to society would be splurging on green cleaning products, she would have scoffed in their face over a Long Island Iced Tea and a plate of blue corn taquitos. She had once been driven like all of them, logging the long work hours, hanging out at Maxwell's Plum, and claiming a quarter-share in the Hamptons. Before Chuck, she had shared an East Side railroad apartment divvied into four sleeping spaces barely large enough for a hammock. One roommate locked in a banker at a blue chip firm and was rarely seen or heard from. Another aspired to become a rare arts trader and ran out on her rent with a wavy-haired sculptor from Siena. Her third roommate, of course, had married the conductor.

Paula nudged the bedroom door open with the roaring edge of the machine. Lucy was probably crafting some culinary *pièce de résistance* even as Paula pushed the damnable vacuum cleaner. Sometimes it was almost as easy to detest Lucy as it was to adore her.

Click. The gears and spinning beater cranked shut to merciful silence. Missy's bed was unmade. It looked like she had slept on top of the pile of crumpled sheets, stuffed animals, half-open books, and the hand-knitted quilt her grandmother had made for her tenth birthday. A week's worth of clothes tumbled from the comforter like a calved glacier. Paula cleared a path into the room. She pulled the gingham curtains wide open, allowing the sunshine to penetrate the streaked windows. She smudged her fingers squeakily at the glass. They had not been washed since they had let the maid go. She had lost that argument after Chuck's last budget-slashing meeting. Easy for him to wield the red pen. Could he have found a vacuum cleaner bag in the house if his life depended on it? She sighed and straightened some papers on the desk.

Missy had not yet found her center of gravity. She had made the JV track squad her freshmen year, but that had been more of a lark than a passion. She excelled at math and numbers, something Paula could relate to, and her science grades had netted her honors placement in her sophomore year. Now, as a junior, she and all her friends were starting to think about colleges. The topic was off limits for Chuck. When Paula had brought it up recently over drinks at California Pizza Kitchen, he had made an off-color joke about the career benefits of Missy's getting knocked up by the son of a neighborhood hedge fund guy. Paula left the pin in that grenade. Her daughter was fresh-faced and guileless, completely out of the loop when it came to the uncertain times that roiled their home. Chuck was becoming insufferable and there wasn't a thing Paula could do about it. It made her long for the days when men put on dark suits and went to work and stayed put in their downtown offices until the first microbrew at the Depot Pub. She just wanted her neatly packaged life back. Okay, so maybe homemaking reeked a bit of home economics class circa 1973. Still, it was her fiefdom and damn if she needed Chuck following her around 24/7 telling her how to do things.

Paula unpinned a picture from the corkboard next to the bed. It was a snapshot – an authentic curling relic of film – of Missy and her Dad. She might have been six. It had been the last week of a long ago summer vacation in Maine. There had been canoeing and swimming and waterskiing; grilled hot dogs and watermelon and toasted marshmallows, all consumed al fresco at the end of each lingering day, on the lawn tumbling down to the lake. Paula and Chuck had even stolen a wine-soaked skinny dip under the moonlit sky one balmy evening when they hoped the kids were asleep. Paula smiled softly at the memory of her husband's frat boy ardor. She studied the photo. Chuck was swinging Missy in his outstretched arms, enroute to a flying splash in the deep blue-green waters off the dock. Missy's eyes were bursting with excitement. Chuck's face was tanned and his mouth open wide in an exuberant cry of pure unadulterated love. A moment captured in time. It had been a rollicking end to a fabulous summer. Then they had packed up and made the long drive home to Jersey. The kids went back to school. Chuck went back to work. And a few days later, the unspeakable happened.

For eight long hours Paula had stared at the TV in transfixed horror, searching for her husband in the cloud of bilious smoke rising from the remains of the towers in lower Manhattan. Cell service was jammed beyond use. When six o'clock came and went, she drove over to the Summit train station. Nearly every parking space was still occupied by old Volvos on their last leg, beaters, and second cars awaiting their missing occupants. Days after the tragedy, splotches of cars still remained. Their owners never returned. But Chuck came home.

Paula wiped a tear from her eye and pinned the photo back up. Her children still had a dad. She still had a husband. And a house that desperately needed cleaning before they left for the city. The vacuum roared to life.

- 8 -
NORA COMES CLEAN

Dan was about to explode. If there was any one thing Nora knew, it was the clutching sound her husband made right before the moment of no return. She could hardly complain. A dozen years in and Dan had not lost one iota of interest for her in that department. It took little more than the flint of a single spark to light him up. A touch of the hand. The sight of her in a t-shirt. A Knicks three-pointer could land her on the living room floor with her toes pointed north above his shoulders and the neighbors below thumping furiously at their ceiling with a broom. Sex with Dan was rarely a subtle affair.

She had been attempting to shower.

"Anybody up for conserving a little water?" he had yelled in, peeling off his stinking, drenched running clothes and dumping them in a ball on the floor. Their apartment was so small it was hard to tell the bathroom from the bedroom from the living room, for that matter. At least they didn't have a claw-foot tub in the kitchen any more, like the closet that had posed as their first apartment when they had moved in together after dating for all of three months. Even Dan did not miss their old Alphabet City roach motel. Nostalgia only ran so deep.

"Doing our bit for a greener planet?" Nora replied over the running water, examining a small zit on her chin in the shaving mirror.

"We all have to do our part," he called in.

"You sure this isn't about *your* part?"

Dan pulled the glass shower door open, revealing to Nora what was abundantly clear. If the Internet hadn't turned the adult film industry into a D.I.Y. affair, Dan might have had something. She had to smile. How many wives boasted a husband who still desired them after all these years, as if they had just gotten lucky on a first date?

"Scrub my back?" he asked with a wink.

"Hold yer horses, pardner." She yanked him playfully into the stall and stepped around him.

"Hey."

"Don't move an inch." Nora snuck out from his grasp, dripping a trail across the bathroom floor. She pulled back her wet hair and peered at her iPhone, which she had foolishly left open on the counter next to the sink. *Phewww.* Her obsessive checking was going to get her in trouble. Good thing she had logged out before she hit the shower. She would have had a lot of explaining to do.

She climbed back into the steamed-up stall.

"What the hell was that all about?" Dan asked from under the showerhead.

Nora scooped a gob of shampoo from his foaming head and applied it generously where it counted with her slippery fingers. Dan, reliably, forgot entirely about what he had just asked.

For all the accumulated complaints she could file based on the checkerboard history that comprised their marriage, Nora could never fault Dan for his passion. Not from the moment he plucked her away from a lesbian poetry reading at

The Nuyorican Cafe and had the wherewithal to call her on what a shallow feminist she made, even as she stomped her foot about issues that back then seemed monumental to her. He listened patiently, buying her glass after glass of Chardonnay as she went on about oppressed gays, the coercive messages of the fashion magazine that she was indentured to at the time, and the great social injustice that women should feel compelled to shave their legs. She had to admit, she had been a bit of a cliché on their first so-called date, but they were good causes and besides, Dan was the one putting the hard word on her.

She had come to the reading with her roommate, a tattooed and militant lesbian performance artist. Plenty of men would have run in the opposite direction, but poor foolish smitten Dan saw beyond it all: the soft juicy center at the middle of her hard core. He didn't take no for an answer then. Was it any great surprise that he had not changed in fifteen years?

Dan kissed her hard beneath the streaming showerhead and then, catching her off guard, spun her around and pressed her hands high against the steamy glass door. Must have been one helluva run, she thought, and then surprised herself with a start as he entered her, the water sluicing down her back. Jesus he could be distracting. How could she be so intent on the potential of her cruelty and in the same breath feel so goddamned good?

Nora knew that Dan was oblivious to the brewing storm that threatened to undermine the tenuous underpinnings of their marital tent. The problem was that the new life Dan had built for himself had become an adjacent wing to anything that seemed remotely appealing to her anymore. As much as it shamed her, she really didn't give a rat's ass whether he caught his big break or not.

If she had to attach a day or a moment – a turning point when it all changed – it was the evening Dan came home and informed her that he had given notice at the events company where he had toiled as a production manager for six years. He was so wrapped up in heralding his own bravery that he failed to notice the deathly silence that came over her. Who gave him a free pass from holding a shitty job like every other struggling artist in New York, anyway? The answer of course was, she did. And he was riding such a high that she could barely get a word in edgewise. He could not stop crowing about his new agent, his new one-man show, his renewed hope that *his* moment had come at last. He said that he needed to keep writing and auditioning, all of this explained over a pricey Pouilly Fuisse that he had brought home just for the occasion. Kathleen – the new agent who actually returned his calls – felt certain that his work would lead to something: a sale, a role, maybe even a production with him as director. She had several Off Broadway heavyweights in mind.

"Real leads," Dan had said, punching his fist on the table. As if she hadn't heard that tired old saw before.

Nora had tried to paste a smile on her face to cover up for her wavering doubt. Was Dan blind to the fact that even if one of these "leads" panned out, it could be years of staged readings and endless rehearsals before a single line of his ever got read before a live audience – not to mention getting paid to act, a detail that sometimes escaped him and left her perennially on the hook for the little things. Like food. The rent. Their health insurance. Had he forgotten that he was a childless, thirty-eight-year-old adult male, and Nora had already left her fertile breeding grounds behind for forty? They'd only been fighting about that unresolved situation since Bloomberg's second term. Forget about starting a family. Even if he got something produced, more likely she'd be dealing with hot flashes than diaper bags before he realized a penny of income. A grown man in acting class with kids half his age, and a one-act in progress that she could not bear to read. Was this why Nora had supported them for all these years? The creative parts of Dan that had seemed so sexy and passionate when they'd first met, all of a sudden left a rancorous taste in her mouth.

"She said," Dan whispered conspiratorially, "this could even lead to a sitcom." Nora tried to hold back her wave of pure revulsion.

"Not a crappy sitcom," he continued, reading her mind. "You know, maybe *Modern Family* or *Parks and Recreation*. And there's all sorts of new stuff coming out on cable. Plenty of it's produced right here in New York." He knew that Nora would sooner flee to the suburbs than set one delicate toe in *Elle-A*.

"That's wonderful, honey," she had offered, trying to muster some tiny modicum of enthusiasm, a quiver of excitement that her actor/writer husband might still have a last gasp chance at getting his elusive break.

That had been two years ago and sure enough – big surprise – they were still hiking five flights of stairs in their pre-war, without-the-glam walkup; still struggling like college paupers to stay one month ahead of the rent on her frozen editor's salary. While the imperturbable Dan was tapping merrily away at his laptop until the wee hours, she was slaving eight hours a day in her cubicle, writing forgettable blurbs about venture capital, innovation and the latest green start-ups for a dying business rag in a dwindling print world. And as far as the elephant in the room? Dan was about as interested in her fertility charts as she was in the Nielsen ratings. She could just sit back and watch as the hands of her biological clock spun into oblivion like the *Sixty Minutes* graphic. *Tick, tick, tick, tick, tick.*

Nora felt Dan's urgency building, his hands clutching at her wrists as their bodies pressed against the rickety shower glass door. She wanted to come too, to let go the way guys did; the way Dan did – that shuddering release that seemed to exorcise men of every last worry in the world, leaving them a snoring shell on an unmade bed. She closed her eyes and concentrated on the moment, trying desperately to push all distraction from her head. The problem was that her focus was bifurcated in the most compromising of fashions. Because while it was impossible to ignore the undeniable pleasure that Dan was providing, in reality, he was the last person on her mind as she finally clenched and came like a cascading waterfall.

- 9 -
NICOLE DROPS OFF

"C'mon kids. Mommy has a train to catch. We've got to go."

"But it's not Dad's weekend," Justin complained.

"He's doing Mommy a favor," Nicole replied. "He's going to be so happy to see you guys," she added hopefully.

Favor was a loose term for it. Most anything Bill did for Nicole was done through clenched teeth at very best. Not that she could blame him.

To the outside world they used words like "amicable" and "good partners." At least she did. It was not always so easy to read her ex, though. At first she could barely tolerate looking him in the eye when they traded the kids. Partly because of her own consuming guilt, and partly because the muted expression on Bill's face could not mask the sheer disgust he felt towards her for putting him in this situation.

The months of couples counseling they had endured after Bill found out about her affair had been an exercise in futility. Maybe at the outset she had harbored some ray of hope that therapy could save the marriage. But mainly she had gone through the motions with an eye toward a rejiggered relationship for the both of them when they came out the other side. She bore no ill will toward her soon-to-be-ex. She hoped they could someday be friends. Despite all they had been through, she still thought of Bill as a good guy. He had other adjectives for her, though. Cheating, conniving bitch for one. She had overheard that sweet *bon mot* one evening when he was on the phone with his best friend, shortly before they had told the children and officially split up. He did not realize she had her ear pressed to the door, eavesdropping. Once a bitch, right?

"Why can't we go with you to see Aunt Lucy in New York?" Emily asked.

"Well honey, because it's a grown-up dinner party. And I'm only going for the evening." *Plus Mommy's bringing her new boyfriend for all her friends to meet and adore and shower her with acceptance, and she's not quite ready to break that news to you kids yet,* Nicole thought to herself. Much less Bill.

Part of their divorce agreement included a paragraph that stipulated that they would not introduce the children to any new partners unless the relationship was deemed serious. How one quantified "serious" was a complete mystery to Nicole. Was documentation required? Photo I.D.? Proof of mutual orgasms? The language of separation, so they were told by their mediator, was driven by a Child's Bill of Rights, which created safety measures designed to prevent hostile parents from parading casual dates in and out like hookers in a fleabag motel. At the time, Bill was so eager to catch Nicole in another act of infidelity that she was ready to sign anything short of agreeing to a court-ordered chastity belt, just to be done with it. In retrospect, the "partners" codicile seemed rather amorphous by definition, but it was inked in blood, so Nicole was abiding by the letter of the law. Gray was as much a secret to Bill and the kids as the sexy intimates she had packed for the weekend in New York.

She placed her overnight bag on the stoop and locked the front door. She took Emily's hand as they headed across

M Street and up the hill towards Bill's new flat. *Daddy's cool apartment*, as Justin referred to it, which gave Nicole a sharp stabbing pain in the gut every time she heard the words. She had only read about thirty books on how to prevent children from taking sides in a divorce. No one had written an effective chapter on how to compete with glassy duplexes stocked to the rafters with cool gadgets and toys.

For the time being, Nicole retained ownership of the house that the kids called home. She and Bill and the lawyers had worked through reams of paperwork outlining when and how she might sell, and how the profits would be divided. The agreement was more complex than the Treaty of Versailles. Nicole had tried one evening to make heads or tails of it, and then succumbed to her third glass of red wine and a sense of resignation that she should just stay put awhile. If things kept sailing along with Gray, there would be plenty of time to sort the real estate out.

"What are you and Daddy going to do tonight?" Nicole asked with feigned cheerfulness as they approached his building.

"Nothing," Justin sulked. Apparently the concept of Daddy's cool new digs was more appealing than the reality.

"What do you mean nothing? Your Dad always has something fun planned."

"We'll probably just rent a dumb movie while he plays on his computer," Emily chimed in.

"His computer?" Nicole asked. "What does Daddy do on his computer?" She knew she wasn't supposed to nose about, but Bill hated computers. The guy was a complete Luddite. He could barely operate an ATM machine and his medical offices had a staff of three just to handle the patient list and insurance needs.

"He looks at pictures of girls," Justin said. "It's gross."

"Dad said not to tell Mommy."

"I didn't."

"You just did."

"Did not."

"Okay guys, enough. Hey, who wants to get an ice cream before I drop you off?"

Girls? she wondered. Either Bill had developed an interest in pornography, which seemed highly unlikely, or her husband had leapt into the fold of online dating. Ex-husband, she reminded herself. For one moment she entertained a thought that might have been a close cousin to jealousy. She was well aware that as the former loving wife and keeper of the domestic bliss, she was infinitely replaceable. But he wasn't allowed to have sex with that person too, was he? Bill was handsome enough, that was for sure. Good lover, great practice, plenty to offer. Maybe he was sowing his wild oats on the weeks when the kids were with her. She wondered what his new taste in women might be. Tall scary intellectuals with edgy glasses and expensive briefcases? Flashy blondes with large breasts and fuck-me pumps? How odd to picture the man with whom you spent the last fifteen years of your life, searching for your replacement. What if he was plying his well-worn bag of tricks with a younger woman? Someone with a three and a zero as the first set of digits in her age? That was too much to bear. She pushed the thought out of her mind as they walked up the steps to the entrance.

"Ring the buzzer, Justin. Go ahead."

Bill had relocated to 18th Street, just off of Dupont Circle. He had been more than gracious when he signed the lease, inviting her to inspect the new home where her children were going to spend half their lives. In truth though, Nicole had barely been through the place. It felt too personal, like she had no business being there. During her cursory walk-through he had shown it off with pride, intent to prove that he was capable of reestablishing himself as the city's most eligible bachelor.

The apartment occupied the top half of a four-story brownstone. It had two ample bedrooms and a study that he had converted into a third. The kitchen had been fitted out in gourmet style with soapstone countertops, retro bar stools, and all the latest appliances. There was even a wrought-iron winding staircase to a rooftop terrace with a fancy gas barbeque and a stellar view of Washington, looking south toward the Monument. It was easy for Nicole to imagine Bill courting a new suitor up there with a tray of expensive nibblies and a bottle of crisp Riesling – the city skyline stretched out before them like a lithograph – as he regaled her with tales from his horror show of a previous marriage. The intercom buzzed them in, interrupting her fantasy.

"Hey."

"Hey," she replied. Their newly adopted language was guttural and monosyllabic. The kids ran to their dad, each giving him an obligatory kiss before they went to co-opt the computer.

"When will you be back?" he asked. The shackles removed, they limited themselves to bare cordiality.

"I reserved the one p.m. Acela, so I'll pick them up around five," Nicole lied. She didn't have a clue when she'd be home. Gray had arranged everything. He was keenly organized and she could imagine him packed and ready in his houndstooth sportscoat, leather overnight bag by his side, awaiting her arrival.

When she saw Bill's groceries for the evening laid out on the small kitchen table, she felt her usual sense of domestic inadequacy. A sack of organic baby carrots lay next to a plump, perfectly browned roast chicken. A pot of water was simmering on the stove. She noted the multi-colored wild mushroom tortellini sitting in a package awaiting rapid immersion into hot water. Two beautifully-coiffed cupcakes sat on a serving plate by the fridge. Did Bill leave the uber-organic Firehook Bakery sack on the countertop just to rub her nose in the fresh pastry? He was well aware of her culinary shortcomings.

"Yummy," Emily crowed, running straight to the cupcake dish. Last night Nicole had gotten hung up at work. When she got home an hour late and spelled the babysitter, she served up a family-sized can of Chef Boyardee ravioli washed down with a box of Oreos. *Bad Mommy.* Try as she did, she could not run and hide. The kids were better off with Bill. She tried to fight back a rampant wave of cavernous self-loathing. Maybe she'd be past it by the time they were in college.

"Come say goodbye to your mother, guys," Bill said. He couldn't be rid of her fast enough.

"Bye Mom." Justin already sported the aloofness of a teenager, years before his time.

"Bye Mommy." Emily clung to her knee and Nicole scooped her up.

"Bye sweetpea."

"Do you have to go?"

"Yes, Mommy has to catch her train. But I'll see you tomorrow. Okay?" She wondered if it ever would get any easier.

"Did you bring Muffie?" Emily asked.

"I did. She's right next to your toothbrush, love." Boy she better have remembered that, Nicole thought to herself.

"Okay. Buh-bye," Emily said in a sad thin voice.

"Buh-bye."

Nicole heard the door lock behind her even before she

had cleared the landing. The cold finality of the clanging deadbolt stuck in her throat like an oversized pill. She walked down the brick steps to the street and paused to look up at the building. The sill was lined with potted plants. Bill had always been a gardener. The window was wide open. "Bye guys," she called up. Her words floated uselessly into the sky.

- 10 -
LUCY'S BEEF

The blade slipped into the blood red meat with the ease of a dagger. Lucy used a paring knife sharpened to a frightening razor edge. It was the ideal tool for larding the filet mignon. She scored the roast, opening each sliver like a paper cut, where she then inserted a wafer thin slice of garlic. She repeated the process in haphazard two-inch grids until she was satisfied that the entire five-pound filet would be infused with the flavor of the roasted garlic once the dry heat did its job. She could almost smell the aroma wafting through the apartment already. Next, she oiled the meat generously, pouring the extra virgin over the roast in a swirling pattern until it ran in a fragrant stream down its sides. She massaged the oil into the flesh, caressing it like a newborn until it was gleaming. She washed her hands under searing hot water and wiped them dry on a floral dishtowel. Then she took her Moulinex pepper mill and peppered the roast with fresh ground on all sides until it formed a cracked coating. Later, right before going into the oven, she would season it with sprinkled scoops of kosher salt. Web debate raged over when to salt one's meat, but she chose to err on the side of caution. There was no greater crime than a dried-out filet mignon roast.

She examined her handiwork, lowering her nose inches above it to inhale the scent of the fresh pepper. Perfect. It would make a fine centerpiece for the meal. She laid a sheet of Saran Wrap over the top and wedged the whole roasting pan into the crowded fridge. It was nearly three o'clock. She would take it out when the first guests arrived so that it would warm to room temperature when it was time to go in. There. Done. What next?

Lionel had gone out at last. He had spent the entire day in the apartment puttering about, listless and without direction. She had finally convinced him to do his raspberry rhubarb pie. Baking suited her husband's temperament. The perfection required, the steps, the choreography – all leading to a piping hot and delicious conclusion. Lionel needed more finished products. Sometimes it seemed to her that his days were a cavalcade of bold attempts and near misses. She'd find his empty coffee cups abandoned everywhere, sitting next to half-read novels and dated magazines. It was as if he was priming his creative pump in any fashion he could muster. Just hours ago he had taken on a grand sorting project in the closet in his study. He had gotten as far as creating a blizzard of papers and folders and notebooks scattered throughout the room, before giving up and stuffing them all back on the highest shelf. She had cajoled him in her sweetest voice to make a dessert for the evening. She just wanted to help him find something – one project for the day that would end with success. And besides, she was going to take hostages if she had to watch him banging off the walls for another second. It made her almost wish she was a football widow.

Lucy got down her largest stainless steel bowl and began mixing the mélange of exotic lettuces she had scored earlier in the day. The salad quickly took on the colors of a Monet. She tore off small pieces of frisee even as she worried about

Lionel's mood. She was truly concerned, when she didn't want to kill him. His tossing and turning nights, the phantom chest pains, and his latest bout with sleep apnea. Or at least that was her diagnosis. He refused to see a specialist, so there was no way to be sure.

"I'm not going out with a mask clamped to my face," he had complained. She had no choice but to sigh and file it under the long list of Lionel's ills, imagined or otherwise. It was his nature to assume the worst. It was hers that he need merely take better care of himself. Both prognoses made him miserable like a child and there was little she could do about it. All those years ago when she'd married a man ten years her senior, she'd barely given a thought to the natural evolution of the aging process. Longevity was not a trait on the paternal side of her family tree. She'd never known either of her grandfathers and she had lost her dad before he even made it to retirement age at the midtown accounting firm where he had labored for so many years. Old men were a foreign concept to her. She wondered if Lionel would last long enough to offer a greater window.

She grabbed a shallot and stripped it of its papery skin in one deft movement. She laid it on the cutting board and did a quick, fine dice, adding a few sprigs of fresh parsley at the end to raise the flavor bar. Maybe it was time for a glass of white wine? She wondered what gems Lionel would excavate from his private collection this evening. She glanced at the clock. He'd probably be home soon. When he did decide to bake, there was a whole rigmarole he went through. Staging *The Mikado* would be easier. Better she finish up her kitchen work so that the maestro could take his space.

She sprayed the field of salad with the finely chopped shallot and herb mix, ground a few twists of fresh pepper on top, and set the bowl aside. The filet mignon was safely resting in the fridge. A collection of cheeses sat out on a board, ripening to the appropriate gooiness. Her work was done. She considered her options. A restorative nap? A long run in the Park? Either seemed a healthy plan. She had three hours until guests. There was time for one other activity, if she wanted. *Bad idea!* What on earth could possibly inspire that? As if she didn't know. It was her usual gluttony for punishment, plus the deep river of angst that ran through her like a ravine. How had they come up with so many medications for depression and not a single pill for pervasive Jewish guilt? She sighed, as she wiped her hands on the towel and put her wedding band back on.

A few moments later, she strolled east on 79th Street, noting how quiet the city was. Late Saturday afternoon and many of the denizens of their upscale neighborhood would still be in the Hamptons. She and Lionel had once considered buying out East. Lionel thought it might be good for the solitude, and his writing. Lucy was enamored of the sweet corn and tomatoes. They had decided in the end, though, that the hassle of fighting the Long Island Expressway every weekend was trumped by their love of Manhattan. They were not really beach people at heart anyway. Lionel's vague interest was an old attachment to the gray blustery days of his youth by the Devon shore, when he and his family would huddle beneath blankets freezing in the North Atlantic mist. And as much as Lucy enjoyed the concept of a clapboard cottage and a walk by the sea, she was fair-skinned. A day at the beach for her involved cover-ups, unwieldy umbrellas, and copious amounts of SPF 45 sunblock. They had settled on the occasional weekend with friends. More would be too much.

The late-day air turned chilly as she rounded the corner onto York Avenue. When was the last time she'd visited her mother? Had it been a couple of weeks? A month? What inopportune impulse had put her on this track? Ruth wasn't expecting her. A large goblet of Chablis and a bath suddenly seemed a very good alternative. Too late. Just the sight of the mighty Weill-Cornell Medical Center set off an emotional chain reaction that sucked her in like a black hole. She continued down the block, lined with one behemoth medical institution after another. The entire breadth of the avenue reeked of sadness and death, she thought, as she entered the arched gateway to the home.

The smell of the Israel Goldstein Center for the Aged overwhelmed her. Most everything about the place did. All of its clientele's well-stocked coffers and trust funds could not belie its true purpose. It was a repository for the elderly, the infirm and the dispossessed – the last place on earth anyone in their right mind would want to end up. Mercifully, very few people who called Goldstein home, were in their right mind. Lucy rode up in the elevator alone.

"Where are my teeth?"

Lucy heard her mother's voice before she entered the room. Somehow, in her advanced dementia, Ruth Kaminsky had gradually returned to the old country. Her accent had grown so strong Lucy half expected her to start muttering in Polish.

Lucy poked her head in the door.

"Afternoon Mrs. K." Harriet was the floor assistant on duty this afternoon. She had been with the nursing home for two years now, a kindly face in a clinical world. Few of the attendants lasted more than six months. Lucy rued the day Harriet might choose to move on.

"Hello Harriet," Lucy said, coming all the way in. Her mother did not even look up.

"Who stole my teeth?"

"She's having a bit of a hard day," Harriet whispered. "Do you want to wait outside while I get her ready?" Normally Lucy called ahead. Maybe her impromptu visit wasn't such a swell idea.

"No. I don't have much time."

"Where are my teeth?"

Lucy winced. It never grew easier, hearing the sound of her mother bellowing like a homeless old woman on a subway bench.

"There you go, Mrs. Kaminsky. Your teeth are right here." Harriet helped her put them in.

"I look terrible."

"You look lovely, dear. Let me comb your hair."

Lucy leaned against the industrial green wall of the room while she waited for Harriet to finish. She felt her fist involuntarily clenching and unclenching. Why had she come?

"Okay Mrs. K. I'll leave you with your Mom." Harriet gestured Lucy closer and then quietly slipped out the door. Lucy slid an easy chair up close to her mother's bed.

"Hi Mama."

"Who are you?"

"It's your daughter, Mom. I'm Lucy." She tried not to flinch.

"They steal."

"Who steals, Mom? What was stolen?"

"My ring. They stole my wedding ring."

"No Mama, no one stole. I have it safe at home."

It was true, though. No matter it was such a fancy place. The attendants still had a tendency to pick up any bracelet, brooch, or accessory that had a lick of value. Even Ruth's crocheted wool sweater with the mother-of-pearl buttons that Lucy had made for her in a fit of craftsman-like pique, had gone AWOL. It was heartbreaking, but within a few moments, whatever Ruth once remembered was lost. Her memory was a skipping record, a detailed diary of events going back eighty years, yet she was unable to retain one iota of what had happened five minutes ago.

Lucy clasped her mother's gnarled knuckles in her own manicured hands. The arthritis had left Ruth's fingers atrophied, the skin wrinkled and flapping like a poorly fitted glove.

"Where's your father?"

Lucy sighed and rested her Mom's hands back in her lap. "He's not here anymore, Mama. Papa's gone."

"I want to go home."

"I know." Lucy adjusted a stray wisp of her mother's gray hair. She stroked her cheek. It felt paper-like and foreign, as if this person could not be related to her. She and her siblings had fought for years over her care. Her brother Ira in Philadelphia, and Linda in Chicago, had plenty to say. But they were hundreds of miles away. It was not their problem. First, the decision to offload the rambling old house they had grown up in. And then later, as Ruth's mental health deteriorated, the painful truth that she could not live alone.

"Who are you?" Ruth repeated.

"I'm Lucy."

"You have to speak up. I can't hear. They stole my hearing aids."

Lucy could see the hearing aids in place. Every visit was the same. They stole my slippers. My robe. My watch. *My soul*, Lucy thought.

"It's me, Mom. Lucy." She reached into the drawer in the night table and pulled out a thick red composition book. The latest drive-by therapist from the home had suggested that the kids and grandkids write to Ruth whenever they visited. A small offering to the gods of dementia to slow the complete erasure of what little was left in her misfiring cortex. Lucy and her siblings had nearly filled the notebook over the course of a year. Lucy wondered if her mother had ever turned a page. She opened it to the latest entry.

"I'm your son Ira, Mom," Lucy read aloud. "I have three children. Andrew, Jamie and Rachel. We live in Philadelphia. Deborah sends her love." The letters were large and blocky. When was her brother last in town? Lucy wondered. He hadn't even bothered to call.

Ruth stared out the window across the street into the verdant gardens of the hospital. Lionel had pulled major strings to get her a room with a view. Lucy placed the book in her mother's lap. It lay there as Ruth looked away.

"Mama. Mom?" She did not respond.

Lucy got up from her chair and fluffed Ruth's pillow. She found the switch to the hospital bed and raised the back with a brief staccato burst. She propped her mother up and then with a dainty little step, hopped up right alongside her. She settled on top of the blankets and held the book up. "Look Mom. See? All of your children have been writing you."

No response. It was like speaking to an infant. Lucy took the pen and wrote slowly as her mother stared off into space. She read to Ruth in a clear, unbroken voice. "I am your daughter Lucy. We live in New York. Lionel and Isaac send their love."

"Who's Lionel?" Ruth asked.

"Lionel is my husband, Mama."

"Where are your children?"

"I only have one child, Mom. Isaac. He's off at college."

Ruth stared at her with such a burning sense of unexpected clarity that Lucy wondered if she was about to get a lecture. It would be just her luck, for her mom to pull from the mosaic of her splintered darkness, some long-ago shortcoming that Lucy had finally overcome in therapy. Time to bring this cheerful visit to its conclusion.

Lucy took the open red diary and wrote again on the bottom of the lined page, in large, impossible-to-miss letters. "I love you, Mama. Your daughter Lucy."

Ruth stared at the page, then gazed at Lucy with a confused look. "Who are you?" she asked, the inflection of her voice rising like a melody.

Lucy sighed and closed the book. Clearly, that was a question she could not answer.

- 11 -
LIONEL'S PIE

He found the raspberries organized in pint boxes at the far end of the fruit section, past the burnished Gala apples, Anjou pears and champagne grapes. Butterfield's produce was immaculate. Lionel enjoyed the pristine displays of star fruit from Malaysia, pomegranates from North Africa, and kumquats from China, laid out in splendid exotic glory each morning as if a travelogue of dusty barefoot natives had handpicked every last piece for the exclusive greengrocer's stuffy clientele. He knew he was violating the locavore movement, the carbon footprint movement, and probably several nations' child labor laws to boot, but Butterfield's was close and Lionel's world required that these days. A longer journey was daunting. It required planning and forethought, mental tools that seemed to have abandoned him of late. Lucy had been pushing for a psycho-pharmacological assessment on top of everything else, but no way was he going down that psychotropic road. Give in there and you might as well throw in the creative towel.

He filled both hands with as many pints of fresh berries as he could. The pretty little boxes boasted roots from an orchard in New Jersey. At least he'd be able to face Dan without mounting a verbal defense of his pie's heritage. He found his way to a slatted crate overflowing with rhubarb, and stuffed several thick-veined stalks under his arms. Maybe one more to be safe. He reached down with the berries precariously cradled between his elbows and tried to nab a stalk. The pint boxes collapsed between the pressure of his hands and tumbled down, followed by his entire crop of rhubarb.

"Shit!"

"Hi Lionel."

He looked up from the floor where he had sunk to his hands and knees, his face as red as the sea of berries he was trying to scoop up. "Hi, uhhh—."

"Marge," she reminded him. "Spenser's Mom."

"Yes, yes, how is dear Spenser?" Without Lucy by his side he could barely remember his own name, much less that of the mother of one of Isaac's friends.

"Spenser is fabulous," she said, crouching down to help Lionel minimize the disaster.

"Bowdoin?" Lionel inquired, wishing he could disappear into the mottled linoleum tiling of the floor.

"Arizona State."

"Of course. Please forgive me. It's hard to keep track."

"Not at all. How's Isaac doing up at Cornell?" she asked. He noticed her shopping basket was as orderly as a vegetable patch.

"Great," Lionel said gathering up the rhubarb. He wondered what store policy was. He couldn't just put all the soiled produce back on the stand, could he? "Absolutely fabulous. Better than his clumsy father, as you can see."

He missed his son, Lionel thought, waving toodaloo with two fingers to Marge. Isaac had been the unpredicted gift to his unexpected courtship. To have found someone as carefree and playful as Lucy, and then, in spite of his deepest fears, produce Isaac? They had nearly not wed, he and his beautiful headstrong Minerva, she was so apoplectic over his unwillingness to father a child. He had been wavering and unsure, plagued with doubt. Lucy was agog over the illusion of nappies and prams and holidays in London. She did not know the half of it, his family's DNA. You didn't have to dig deep to find a Shakespearean cast of horse thieves, gypsies, drunks, depressives and misfits. Dysfunction in a test tube. It was one thing to crow about her fascinating distant in-laws from Cornwall and Cambridge and the north of Scotland. It was another to have known them. How could he tell his beguiling Manhattan vixen that while he could masterfully lead an orchestra or compose a symphony, he was deathly afraid of a brood.

Lucy had all but coaxed the baby out of him, amidst a smokescreen of sexy entreaties and her innate willfulness. He remembered the day they brought Isaac home. Lucy, forever organized like a field marshal, had left him alone for a few moments with the carefully wrapped infant in a wool blanket while she unpacked from her hospital stay. He had examined the fresh-faced bundle of flesh and blood at arm's length, gazing upon it until Lucy finally returned and found him holding their son out in his hands like a neatly folded burrito.

"Honey," she had asked. "Are you all right?"

"What do I do with him?" he had replied, and truly, he had no clue. No one in his family ever did. Look how they all turned out. Could she blame him?

And yet over the years, as Isaac had morphed into a toddler, a child, a teen, Lionel had learned to wear his parenthood like a comfortable tweed coat, something to be slipped on at short notice with little effort. He was there when it was easy: the soccer match, the violin recital, the lazy Sunday morning breakfast as he read his *Times* over French press coffee. He doled out sage, fatherly advice on after-school clubs, summer camps and college applications, peeking out from his horn-rimmed bifocals in the evening while he enjoyed a novel and WQXR. Lionel had done none of the heavy lifting. That all went to Lucy. Early on, when she had lobbied for another child amidst the tyrannical months of sleepless nights, fold-up strollers and pre-nursery school testing, he had balked at the very notion. Wasn't their plate full enough? Lucy's fuse had burned hot and bright at his refusal, but it had been a short-lived debate. They had moved past it like a bad weekend. One child, Lionel had sighed with relief, was just enough. He cherished Isaac like a perfectly drawn out single violin note and saw no reason to muddy the score with additional harmonies. His stubborn refusals seemed a lifetime ago. Of course now he sometimes wondered whether Lucy had been right in the first place. Ever since Isaac had left the rambling apartment, he could not have been lonelier.

Lionel stared at his basket full of ruined produce. Would he be arrested if he just shoved it under a shelf and ran from the store? An assistant manager interrupted his train of thought, relieving him of about a bushel of squashed berries without a question asked. Lord knows Butterfield's could afford it. Lionel nodded an embarrassed apology before fetching a new basket. This was why he was better off holed up in the flat all day. It limited the damage he could do. He regathered his goods, mentally calculating the cost of the ingredients. It would have been cheaper to stroll over to the patisserie on Madison and score a couple of fresh homemade pies. Easier too. They'd be better than anything he could concoct. But Lucy would be disappointed. For reasons far beyond his ken, she still enjoyed his company in the kitchen on a Saturday afternoon. The thought was tantalizing. And besides, baking a pie would give him something quantifiable to do before guests came. Which was infinitely better than returning to his echoing, barren study.

He paid at the checkout and exited to the avenue. His mood perked up as he headed towards home. Lucy would be back putting the finishing touches on her feast. There was plenty of time to mix up a batch of martinis. Riding up in the elevator, he felt a stirring for his lovely wife – a bit of unresolved business from dawn. Not an unpleasant development at all he decided as he fumbled for his keys.

"Lucy?"

He wandered the apartment in search of his quarry. Nothing. She was nowhere to be found. His spark of interest quickly ignited to the familiar tinderbox of jealousy and mistrust. "Damnit," he cursed out loud. He leaned heavily against the marble-covered radiator by the large living room picture window. He stared out at the building across the street. Due north. Thirty blocks short of Harlem. It was nearly four o'clock. Could she be up there, again? He clenched his eyes shut. It was more than he could bear. Why not just confront her?

He rumbled over to the bar and uncorked a bottle of sherry. He could not even be bothered with ice. The thick viscous liquid splashed over the rim of the crystal glass. He did not care. The first sip burned going down. Even so, he felt the edge fading as he drew deeply again.

- 12 -
DAN'S TERROIRE

If there was any one thing Dan could bank on, it was sex. Loved it as a kid, locked in the bathroom all by himself. Loved it as a horny teenager on the bench seat of his father's Buick sedan. Couldn't get enough of it in college with all those expressive, winsome girls in the theatre department. Give him a stage and he was in his element. A fox in the chicken coop. It was amazing what a constant sex was in his life. His romp with Nora in the shower had the effect of topping off what had been a perfect day so far. He knew he was a rare creature: a man who still craved his wife with wanton abandon. It wasn't that he didn't notice other women. New York was a smorgasbord for any guy with a wandering eye, rich with temptation at every corner, every subway car, every pizza shop. His highly tuned radar was no secret to Nora. She loved to tease him about it. "You'll dump me like a bad habit when you get your big break," she had joked for years.

That was where she was wrong. Of course he'd dodged some interesting bullets. Didn't everyone? That was why you lived in the city. The never-ending merry-go-round of faces and bodies, stolen glances and close calls. It was the human interaction that fueled him: his writing, his stories, the acting.

Just recently, there had been the woman in his acting class, Liza with a Z. She was a software executive in a go-nowhere career, which she had chucked before the economy chucked her. It was not an uncommon tale. People were running scared. She had taken her buyout and sunk it into a twelve-week crash course and damn, she was good. Dan had done a scene with her from *The Glass Menagerie*. She was a snarky Mary Louise Parker to his Kevin Bacon, and the overtures were clear. That was the thing about New York. Women didn't age. The city kept them young, engaged, hungry. His software-executive-cum-actress was vibrant, her eyes charcoal and alive, and when they shared a glass of cheap wine after class, her inviting patter was unmistakable. Except that Dan had no intention of crossing that bridge, because he already had what he wanted. Everything but that one elusive break. And that was coming as sure as his one-act was percolating along. He could feel it in his bones.

He strode down Broadway, fighting his way past the crowd elbowing to get into Zabar's. At 74th Street he zigzagged across the avenue, barely avoiding a careening cab.

"I'm walking here," he said, doing his best Ratso Rizzo as he sidestepped an extraordinarily harried-looking mom pushing a stroller the size of a shopping cart. Boy was he glad not to have that disaster on his plate yet. It was the one nagging sore spot with Nora. The topic he jumped through hoops to avoid. In time, he thought. Two sounded nice. Maybe even a trio. He could picture them like *My Three Sons*, lining the front row of the Stadium on a summer's afternoon. Soon enough.

Inside Beacon Wine & Spirits, the glassy rows greeted him like a bacchanalian choir. He made his usual foray into the stacked crates of discounted wines, no particular destination in mind. Budget dictated his mission. That was the price he paid for pursuing his craft. He read through the wine descriptions pasted on elegant card stock above each selection. He picked up a late-model French Zin. *A hint of mulberry and oak combines earthy tones with a strong blackberry finish. $7.99.*

Hmmm, not bad. Would Lionel know it was swill? Did Dan really give a damn? Impressing the majestic Lionel Birnbaum, with his mastery of music and prodigious wine acumen, would require a lot more of an investment than Dan was prepared to make. He moved down the row. A South African pinotage caught his eye. A tasteful giraffe stood guard over the etched vineyard on the bottle. *This West Cape varietal has all the wildness of African plain grasses, cooled by the South Atlantic mists. Hints of blueberry, licorice and dark chocolate make for a robust excellence that layers nicely with fish or fowl.*

Who writes this crap? he wondered. Could true oenophiles detect the good stuff from the rot in a blind tasting test? Maybe he'd pick up a cheap bottle and pawn it off on everyone as a major vintage. He fought back the trace of jealousy that always nipped at him when he had to deal with his best friend's husband. Lionel wasn't a bad bloke. And he treated Lucy like a prince. It wasn't her fault that he'd composed the world's most obnoxious and unforgettable score. Dan should have been so lucky. A couple of cases of good Bordeaux stowed in a West End Avenue two bedroom with river views, purchased off the fat of a multi-picture deal, would surely do wonders for Nora's mood. She had been so pissy of late that she hadn't even mentioned the thumping of her biological clock for months.

"Can I help you?" A sales associate zeroed in on Dan's daydream, his just-got-laid high starting to fade with the cost of good grape.

"I don't know. I'm looking for something impressive for

someone who can't be impressed."

"I hear you man. What's your top end?"

Dan shrugged, the universal language of the eternally stretched.

"Follow me. I got you covered."

Dan gave chase as the clerk hightailed it out of discount-land and into the rows of privileged wine real estate.

"Here. This is the ticket."

Dan examined the bottle. No red pickup trucks or grazing giraffes on this *boteille*. Instead, a tasteful etching of a black and white chateau accompanied by some very thin type with a name that he could not pronounce. Just the font looked expensive.

"2000 St. Emilion Grand Cru. Not a well-known year, but a damned fine one. Collectors will be holding it, but you can drink it now. Extremely robust. Ya nearly need a spoon to drink the stuff."

2000. Year of the Subway series, Dan thought. "How much?"

"Forty five."

Holy crap. That was more than he and Nora spent on groceries for the week.

The clerk looked at him. Dan had willingly been led into these waters. Was he going to sink or swim? Every bone in his body said dog paddle for safety, pronto. He handled the bottle like a Stradivarius. No gummy Price Slasher sticker smeared on. It hailed from its own rack, instead of a cheap balsa wood display crate. Dan possessed a built-in sense of extreme economic self-control. He could snoop out a discount at the local grocery store a mile away. He bought generic raisin bran and their cupboard was crammed with Ronzoni, his favorite spaghetti, stockpiled at five for three dollars. He'd once considered starting "The Ramen Blog," a foodie primer for starving artists. While his fellow actors dreamt of salvation from their monthly rent, Dan longed for little more than enough scratch to buy a case of Heineken – with cash – at will.

He fingered the heavy stock label on the bottle. "What the hell, why not," he said at last. He was feeling emboldened by his run, the sex, and the thought of a primo Lucy dinner to come. He carried his purchase to the front of the store.

"Gift wrap?" the checkout woman asked, ringing him up.

"Huhhh?" Dan was too busy watching the credit card machine, waiting for the printout paper to engage. He prayed they had paid the bill on time. The tape started to spit out. He breathed a sigh of relief.

- 13 -
GRAY TAKES STOCK

The three p.m. Acela raced across the railroad bridge spanning the inner estuary of the Chesapeake Bay. The sparkling blue waters stretched into the distance. There were few boats out. What a shame. If Gray had a boat this was precisely the kind of day he'd be on the water. He wondered if Nicole liked to sail.

She had dozed off on his shoulder, her straight long hair tumbling over his sleeve. She wore a sequined knit sweater over her black cocktail dress. A snapshot of simple elegance. An hour before, she was anything but. She had pressed him back into the narrow vestibule of his apartment entranceway and fallen to her knees, administering to him in a fashion that none of his previous wives had shown a glimmer of interest in for years. The price of marriage, he had mused quietly to himself later on the taxi ride to Union Station. Who could sustain? He was perfectly happy in safe, distant orbit with the bright star that Nicole had become in his life – supernova to his scholarly, staid existence. The spontaneity of their stolen moment was only heightened by the fact that he lived in a five-story, ten-unit building. Nicole was unperturbed by the notion that any neighbor could have walked in on them, interrupting an act that he believed might still be illegal in several southern states. He smiled at the thought of it. They had nearly missed their train, not that he was complaining. Nicole made him feel young and alive in ways he had long ago lost track of. He felt like he had won the lottery. He wondered how her friends would feel about him. Apparently tonight was *hail, hail the gang's all here*.

They had met under the most unprofessional of guises. Nicole was the kind of work-related sand trap that Professor Graydon Barnes had assiduously avoided. He had agreed to appear as the resident liberal on a bombastic *Nightline* panel after an especially controversial Supreme Court decision had rattled the mainstream media. Gray preferred to voice his outspoken opinions through the classes he taught at Georgetown, or in longer form, through his books – the latest of which had wormed its way up to number 19 on the *New York Times* Best Seller List. He found the medium of television fleeting and reactionary – a rampant form of hypocrisy to the very thesis of his work. The purloined sound byte, the digital blink the next day should you say anything quote-worthy, and then the idea was lost, decimated in a sea of misinformation. Gray hated doing TV. But his agent and publicist loved it, so when the detached voice from ABC News begged him to appear on the segment, he reluctantly agreed. She set up his appearance as a live remote from the M Street offices of the network. He need merely show up.

"Professor, I am thrilled to meet you," Nicole gushed, shaking his hand, all the while dragging him forcibly into the studio. "Your book was pure can't-put-down good."

"Please," he protested. "I already agreed to be here. Enough."

"No, swear to god. I read it in a night."

"I had hoped my life's work was a bit denser than that."

"I do a dozen bookings a week. I usually have an

assistant prepare notes. Believe me, you rated."

He pretended to be annoyed at the compliment, a habit that perpetually miffed Angela – wife number three – to no end. Theirs had been a short-lived affair. He hadn't even removed her hair products from their formerly shared bathroom, before she hightailed it out to San Francisco to seek her fame in Silicon Valley. She quickly hooked up with a VC legend with a penchant for Formula One racing and his own private jet. She had faxed the hurried divorce papers from the air somewhere between SFO and Monte Carlo.

Unshackled from any last vestiges of nuptial distraction, and with both his daughters and his son from the previous marriages grown up, Gray was finally cut loose to finish his seminal work, which was then published to surprising and rapid acclaim. Overnight, he had risen in the ranks of academia straight into the national dialogue. Angela always said he enjoyed the sound of his own voice. Clearly this brash ABC producer with the coal black eyes agreed, though in a far more pleasant manner.

"You killed," Nicole said afterwards, as they waited outside on M Street for his car service to return him to Georgetown.

"How could you tell between all the shouting?"

"It was your pregnant pause after Beckwith went berserk. That look you gave him was a flash of pure brilliance. I nearly peed myself in the control room."

"You did?"

"Trust me. It's all in the moment."

The Town Car pulled up. Neither made a move.

"I should be finishing my notes for class," Gray announced. "This obscene investment of time is going to put a major dent in the trajectory of tomorrow's youth."

"Maybe you haven't capitalized properly on your

investment."

The car window rolled down. "Barnes to 31st Street NW?" the driver asked.

They both reached for the door simultaneously. Their hands brushed. Nicole held on for a moment longer than was called for.

"I bet you could do that lecture in your sleep," she said.

"Are you this bold with all your guests?"

"Only the left-leaning ones."

"You have impeccable tastes."

"It's my moral prerogative."

Gray slipped his glasses down to the end of his nose, peering at her like a minister over his lectern. "There's a tavern on upper Wisconsin I go sometimes to gather my thoughts."

"I get off at midnight," Nicole said. "Think you'll have them gathered by then?"

The next stop will be Wilmington, Delaware. Please be careful of the space between the car and the platform. Wilmington, Delaware, in three minutes. The high-speed train slowed precipitously. Nicole stirred on his shoulder. "Mmmmm, you smell good."

"So it's the pheromones?" he said pulling her close.

"It's everything. You suppose Acela bathrooms have a settee in them?"

"Nicole, I'm forty-eight, not seventeen. I need more than an hour to recharge my batteries."

"I bet I could do something about that," she said, one hand finding its way to the soft tropical wool of his trousers.

Amazingly, he thought, she could.

- 14 -
NORA ONLINE

Okay, this was crazy. Dan was all of fifteen feet away, preening wildly through the open bedroom door, and here she was: skulking about on the computer, one screen minimized to Google, all the while scanning her inbox for a message. Should he walk out into the living room, she'd have to hide the evidence in a flash. That was, if their stupid four-year old PC didn't freeze up with the damning evidence painted on the screen. Ever since Dan had quit his day job, they had been trimming costs so severely that he'd refused to replace their relic of a desktop. "So it takes a few extra seconds to download a jpeg," he had told her.

Sure. A few extra seconds of processing time and if Dan caught a glimpse of what Nora was processing, the next stop would be divorce court. *As if we have anything to split*, she thought. *You take the Visa debt, I'll assume the MasterCard.*

It hadn't always been that way. They'd been riding such a wave of hope when Dan had landed the John Malkovich role in the David Mamet play going up in Chicago. Okay, so Malkovich had already made his imprimatur on it. And it wasn't Steppenwolf, it was an offshoot company. Still, her friends and her mother had actually heard of the play, even if they couldn't identify the name of Dan's character. And it was work. Paid work as an actor, with a contract and benefits and a regular paycheck.

She hadn't been eager to leave New York and her thriving network of journalistic connections behind. It had taken years to establish herself as a top-drawer business writer, and her *Vanity Fair* piece had all but cemented her place in the pantheon. It had hit at precisely the right time – a profile of a 90s rogue executive whose sentence came down on the same day as the magazine's release date. The buzz had been incredible and at last she was getting noticed for what she had always aspired to be: a serious writer. Still, Dan was so enthusiastic and the Web did make it possible for her to work from anywhere. Besides, a steady paycheck plus benefits had been such a stranger in their lives. For the first time since they had wed, Dan would finally be pulling his weight.

Armed with a fourteen foot U-haul that housed all their cherished belongings with room to spare, and her laptop crammed with the promise of assignments, Nora pasted on a brave smile as they lurched onto the potholed Henry Hudson Parkway and then west out of New York.

You can focus on your good stuff every day, Dan had promised when he was selling her on the sea change that his break was going to wreak on her carefully guarded routines.

Well, she thought, two months after the towers of Lake Shore Drive had loomed in their windshield. The writing part had been on the money. Since she didn't know a soul in Chicago, there was little more to do than write – or at the very least, beat herself up with guilt over how she wished she felt like writing. She missed the jostle of the subway, the crowded streets of midtown, the office drones sneezing on her food at the salad bar every day. The lack of daily misery that Manhattan provided had left her creative side wallowing in a vast, uninspired rut. She was so lonely she ached.

While Dan made new friends with his cast and crew, she wiled away the hours at the local Starbucks, scratching away at her novel, her poetry, and the increasingly rare magazine assignment that emanated from New York. For all the promise of the connected world, her presence on the Street had become as dated as a Rolodex. Her hard-fought connections at *Fortune* and *Forbes* and *The Times* withered on the vine, while Dan performed Wednesday through Sunday nights and the Saturday matinee. His success should have filled her with joy, and yet she felt if she had to sit through one more excruciating performance, she might just have an embolism. Some wife!

When Dan's theatrical run ran out, the money was two beats behind. Their Chicago debut quickly morphed into a painful drama on a cramped stage with diminishing funds and an out-of-work actor trapped in a go-nowhere script. It was only the residual accolades for her fast fading *VF* piece that garnered her just enough street cred to land an offer back in the city as a beat reporter for the market pages of a second tier magazine. Six months after Dan convinced her to go west for his brilliant career, she had to convince him that his next big break would be in New York. The U-haul was packed in an hour. Eight hundred miles later they barely spoke as the van crossed the George Washington Bridge.

Nora peered through the bedroom door to check on Dan's whereabouts. He stood oblivious in front of their Kmart full-length mirror, one hand cupping his balls as he unabashedly admired his penis. Did they all think they were Michelangelo's *David*, she marveled to herself. *Boys and their manhood.* She double-clicked on her furtive Match.com account and quickly scrolled through her inbox in search of Greg, aka MDnyc84. That was the online moniker of her secret paramour, for who all she knew, was as nefarious and dishonest as she. I mean how could she be sure that MDnyc84 wasn't in the same married boat, leading a dual life on Match.com.

It began as a goof, relaxing in the sauna at Equinox with her gym friend, Sue. It was the one luxury Nora afforded herself, a weekly Hatha class followed by a satisfying sweat. She and Sue had started trading notes about the rigors of marriage, draped in skimpy towels, basting in their woes. Their circumstances could not have been more different. Sue, as best Nora could tell, had it all: banker husband, two tow-headed kids in private school, a Chelsea highrise triplex, and a fulltime nanny to boot. Throw in orchestra seats at the Met and a summer cottage in the Berkshires, and on the surface, comparisons seemed as distant as the rings of Saturn. That was, until the day Sue learned that her loving husband not only provided the moon and the stars for her, but for his lover as well. To make matters worse, the dreaded girlfriend had been comfortably coexisting in a cozy studio walk-up that Sue's husband subletted for her on a shady Greenwich Village side street. For two years! Okay, so Dan's narcissism paled in comparison. Still, the women found plenty of ground to relate.

So far Sue's pending divorce had netted her the triplex, enough alimony to have another half-dozen kids were she so inclined, and the lawyers were still hopeful for the Great Barrington cottage. For all that though, she confessed, meeting a decent replacement guy was a bear.

"Go online," Nora suggested. Wasn't that how everyone was hooking up?

"I can't parade myself around like that," Sue had complained as they perspired alone in the hotbox. "I'm a grown woman. I have kids on Facebook."

"Where else are you going to look?" Nora replied. "You

really want to start hanging out at bars, scoping out Goldman guys on the Upper East Side?"

One evening, after an especially invigorating yoga and sweat, Nora and Sue spread out at a nearby outdoor café with a laptop, salads, and a couple of strong cosmopolitans. With Nora's editorial expertise and Sue's reluctant cooperation, her Match.com profile was born. By the time they were done crafting the words, they were inebriated enough for Nora to shoot away with Sue's expensive digital camera, creating a series of photographs to post. They settled on something vaguely professional, as well as the requisite body shot that revealed Sue's shapely cleavage.

"Completely ridiculous," Sue exclaimed.

"What man could say no?" Nora replied.

In no time at all Sue's dance card was full, which left Nora to amuse herself by scouring the tiny little pictures that Sue forwarded her to check out. Armed with a password, Nora was intrigued by this vast underworld of available single men. When Sue got hot and heavy with Tyler, a starving, hip downtown photographer eight years her junior, Nora's excuse to spy on Match was gone. That was, until one night when Dan was out late at an acting class for the umpteenth time. Lonely and bored, just for the hell of it, Nora logged on to Sue's account for a quick fix.

"Access Denied," she was informed. Apparently Sue had canceled her membership. Nora felt a pang of regret, like an ex-smoker hunting for a pack in a forgotten drawer. Emboldened by a tasty Shiraz, she clicked on the "Create A Free Profile" icon. She scrolled through screen after screen, answering the questions as if she were single. Had she lost her mind? She re-read the fine print three times. There was no payment required for a thirty day trial period. Of course she did not upload a picture. She was drunk, not stupid. What hurt was there in looking?

She clicked on "Register." The home page morphed into the familiar sea of hopeful male faces. A digital banner popped up: "Welcome NORA234." She had used the same heading as her first college computer log-on. That seemed safe. How wrong she was.

"Do you think I look fat, old and tired?" Dan called in from the bedroom.

Nora glanced up from her monitor. Her husband was still ogling his naked physique in the bedroom. She had to hand it to him, he looked good. Cute butt, chest still firm and toned. He had a few sprinkles of gray on his full head of hair that only added to the package. Even his recently exercised member still seemed semi-poised with desire, ready to rack it up again with one touch. Were it only about the sex, she'd be richer than Trump.

"No Dan," she replied. He was more vain than she was. "You definitely don't look tired." He didn't hear a word she said.

She perused her inbox. Nothing new from the enigmatic doctor. She thought about his last communiqué. His words were tempting, without being too forward. Coy with just the right amount of edge. She had responded in kind and left him on a dangling note, the door wide open for him to take it to the next level. There had not been a word since. It had been over a day.

"Hey Nora, did you pick up our dry cleaning?" She heard Dan rummaging around the closet, followed by a rumbling fart.

God marriage was sexy.

"Whups. Found it."

She should just delete her profile, cancel the account,

and stop screwing around. What was she hoping to accomplish? With a couple of quick keystrokes she could end the whole charade. Then, like an addict, she clicked back to Dr. Greg's last message. She re-read it for the 400th time.

"Do you think anyone ever really connects on these websites?"

She pondered his metaphysical inquiry. Were those the words of a sweet, vulnerable guy trapped in a sad and passionless marriage, or an asshole on the make looking to get laid? Over the past couple of weeks she had studied the profiles of several hundred men or more. What would her shrink say about *that*, had they still been able to afford her therapy?

She didn't need to crib together a hundred and sixty bucks for the answer. It was obvious. Nora was hungry. She had a gnawing appetite for something, only she had no idea what. There was only one way to satisfy her craving. She had typed back a five-word reply to MDnyc84. "Call me and find out." She followed her message with the ten digits of her cell phone number and hit send. Since then, it had been radio silence.

Nora glanced at the clock. It was getting late. She could see Dan buttoning his shirt through the open bedroom door. She logged out, cleared her Web history from the browser toolbar, and quit out of the screen. Time to get ready for Lucy's party.

- 15 -
PREP

The last gasp of daylight filtered through the small kitchen window that looked out over the building's airshaft. Its offering was opaque on the best of days. Autumn was definitely on the move, Lucy thought. She rummaged through the cupboard, searching for the panko breadcrumbs. Time to get cracking on the hors d'oeuvres. The night was racing up on her.

"I saw my mother today," she said.

"How is the ol' biddy?" Lionel asked, shooting her a furtive sideways glance from the chopping board, where he was converting stalks of rhubarb into geometrically perfect little squares.

"The same. She's always the same," Lucy replied, fighting for a square inch of counter space. "Jeez, could you have made a bigger mess in here?" As gracious as their apartment was, the kitchen was cramped and narrow, more than ample for one, but inadequate for two to operate inconspicuously.

"You asked me to make a pie. I'm making a pie."

"You couldn't have done a store-bought crust?"

"Why don't I just run out and buy an Entenmann's chocolate cake. That will solve the whole bloody problem."

"What problem, Li. Must it all be so black and white for you?"

"No love," he said, kissing the back of her neck as they touched butts crossing paths. "I'm sorry. It's been a rough day." He didn't bother to tell her why.

"You wrote?" Lucy asked hopefully, as she opened a can of fresh Maryland crabmeat. She had decided at the last moment that one hot appetizer would be fun. When it came to food, she just couldn't help herself. She had opted for an improvised take on a mini crab cake recipe that she had cribbed from the Wednesday *Times* food section. Something vaguely Asian and light, a flavorful opening note to the evening's festivities.

"I tried," he lied. "Tell me about your mum."

"She had no idea who I was," Lucy said. "She said someone stole her teeth."

"Did she at least remember your name?"

"Nope. But I told her we were having a dinner party. And I told her all about you and your work, and Isaac, and the menu, and all our friends who are coming over." Lucy didn't mention what she didn't tell her.

Lionel nodded, as he peeled fresh lemon zest off the thick-skinned yellow fruit, careful not to add a healthy swirl of his own pink flesh. He wiped his hands on a dishtowel and took a sip off a glass he had going. Lucy wandered over and took a sniff. The heady aroma of gin hit her like an updraft. She wondered what number he was on. She lifted the glass and took a snort herself. *If you can't beat 'em.*

"Did you know that my mother used to drink Tanqueray martinis?" Lucy announced. "She liked hers with a single fat green olive bobbing in it."

"Our Ruth on martinis? I find that hard to believe."

"Oh Lionel, she was such a different person back then. I

think everyone was. People actually had fun."

"Yes, the good ol' days."

"There was this night I remember. We were just little. My Dad was still alive of course, and my folks were having guests over. It was snowing like mad out. That was back when it used to snow in New York."

"Excuse me, dear." Lionel carved out a small space next to Lucy's cutting board. He took the flour and covered the soapstone surface in a fine dust. He laid a mound of butter dough on top and started to gently knead it. "Go ahead then. Sorry."

"Not at all." Lucy emptied the crabmeat into a bowl and began separating out the stray bits of cartilage. "They had these best friends – the Warrens and the Golds – who always came over on Saturday nights. My Mom would whip up the most elaborate meals: Steak Diane and Chicken Cacciatore. Lobster Newburg. We'd be in our jammies before everyone arrived. We'd watch TV upstairs. *Mary Tyler Moore* and *The Brady Bunch* and *The Bob Newhart Show*. And when Greta chimed the silver dinner bell – can you believe we actually had a maid who rang a bell to call the guests? – we kids would all come running downstairs and say g'night. We called everyone Mister and Missus. Or maybe it was Aunt and Uncle. I can't even remember."

Lucy reached around Lionel and opened the fridge, pulling out a Pyrex bowl with a dozen plump shrimp. She peeled them in the sink, washing the diaphanous skins from her fingertips under the cold water. Lionel began to roll his dough out into the ragged flat makings of a crust. Their movements were as practiced as two moons in orbit around one another.

"That night," Lucy said, plopping a handful of shrimp onto the cutting board, "I can still remember Mike Warren dusting the snow off his fedora when he came in. God, men looked so nice in hats. I always thought he was handsome."

"Going for the older men even back then."

"Silly," she said, pinching Lionel's butt cheek. She got out her nine-inch Wusthof and started dicing the shrimp with practiced deft strokes. "Everyone was cocktailing in our den. I'm sure you could picture it. Long retro bench couch, green shag carpeting, overwrought black and white Marimekko hanging on the wall. Come to think of it, I suppose it wasn't retro back then. Anyway, they'd be listening to Sinatra and Count Basie and Judy Garland. We'd sneak downstairs and peek in and everyone had big tinted cocktail glasses and they all smoked. It was so sexy."

"A family of drunks after my own heart."

"Yes, you would have loved them. Usually we had to go to bed when they started their dinner. But for some reason that night we were allowed to stay up. Maybe it was the snowstorm. I don't know. But the booze was flowing and I remember hearing this ruckus from the dining room, so I snuck out to the landing. The plates were left half-full on the table and there was a cold draft blowing through the open front door and all the grownups were out on the street in their cocktail dresses and jackets and ties. Guess what they were doing?"

"Tell me."

"They were sledding!" Lucy's eyes sparkled and her smile widened at the thought. "Our driveway was on a steep hill and the women had thrown the men's overcoats over their dresses like shawls and they were taking turns flying down the driveway on our Flexible Flyers. And you know what I remember most?" Lucy put down her chopping knife, as if she could feel the chill air even in the warmth of the kitchen. Lionel raised his eyebrows in a bushy question mark. "My

Mom's laughter. It was like a bell. She was so young back then. God, she must have been forty. And she was thin and beautiful and she dressed in skinny bright dresses and oh, Li, she laughed and laughed that night. The streets were all quiet and tamped down and there was no sound except for the scraping of the sleds, and my Mom's voice drifting through the snowy sky."

Lionel put one finger gently on the side of Lucy's crooked nose, leaving a trail of piecrust flour. He adored her nose. He called it her beak. He adored her. "I'm trying to picture your mother sledding down a driveway, drunk on martinis," he said.

"I know. Hard to believe." Lucy turned back to the cutting board and dumped the chopped shrimp into the stainless steel bowl with the lump crabmeat. She took a mound of scallions and sliced the thicker onion-y parts on the bias, tart little sprigs to accompany the round crisp greens. Next, she made hay of a fat bunch of cilantro, raking the larger twigs out as she shredded the leaves. Lionel watched from the sidelines, his wife the mini-cuisinart.

"You're very appealing when you cook, you know."

Lucy picked up a large bottle of Nam Pla sauce and shook it several times into the bowl. Then she dumped in the plate of panko breadcrumbs and spooned in a little mayonnaise and started molding the mix into tiny little puff crab cakes. She placed each one delicately on a thin baking pan.

"Done." Lucy drew a long line of Saran Wrap from the dispenser and covered her creation. "I'm going to get ready. Do you need any help with the pie?"

Lionel surveyed his disaster in the kitchen. "No, it's not as dire as it appears. I just need to roll out the dough a bit, zest a few more lemons, and add the rhubarb and berries.

Shouldn't be a bother at all. I'll clean up, Luce. Don't worry.
Go. Relax. I've got it covered."

An hour later, Lionel stared at his reflection in the glass of
the framed Gold Album in the study. The scent of baking pie
wafted through the apartment. He scrutinized himself: the
new architect-style glasses Lucy had picked to update his
image. The black silk tennis shirt that had set him back $340
at Paul Stuart, tucked into his charcoal wool trousers. Lucy
said he looked young and intellectual. He simply felt like an
impostor. A mime for the articulate, gesticulating madly
about what he might do, were he ever able to squeeze out
another intelligent note.

Night had fallen and the study was illuminated in pale
yellow like a corner bar. Lionel walked over to the piano and
tapped idly on the keys with one finger. *The rain in Spain falls
mainly on the plain.* My god he had fooled the lot of them. Lucy
most of all. Dear, sweet precious Lucy. She had bought into
the whole act. His eee-oh-so British accent. The confidence
of his conductorship when they had first met.

Lionel got up from the piano and walked over to one of
the built-ins, where he picked up a tarnished silver frame he
kept on the ledge. It was a photograph of his older brother
and him. It had been taken centuries ago. Charles was
different than Lionel, more adventurer than intellect. How
Lionel looked up to him. Charles was no poseur. He was the
real talent of the family. He used to belt out Elvis songs with
the guitar he got for Christmas that was nearly larger than he
was. He snuck fags in grade school and joined the jazz club,
and bought Lionel his first pint of bitter at the pub, where he
played a beat-up old Fender in a local rock band. What
Charles lacked in intellectual prowess, he made up for in
sheer charisma. If Lionel was Mozart, Charles was Chuck

Berry. Or so he fancied himself. Lionel always wanted to be like his brother, but he could never keep up. Charles was too fast: with the girls, the music, the drink. Always on the edge, which was precisely where it came to a screeching end – a skid mark on the M1, racing his Triumph motorbike to a gig in Manchester. The police said he was doing 140 kilometers per hour. Fast and painless. Which was a lot more than could be said of their father's demise. That took years under the bottle to kill the pain. Who said suicide had to be a quick affair?

"Lionel, will you button me?"

"Jesus, you scared me."

"Honey, relax. It's just our friends."

He feasted on her with unbridled appreciation. She was tucked like a scythe into a slinky Armani cocktail number that she saved for the most favored occasions. Her feet were still bare, her dainty toes done up in a lacquered burgundy red. Her calves were toned and muscular, like tasty little chops. His Lucy had not aged a bit, not since their early days of dating. Thank God she had left the law behind, Lionel thought. One night at a firm dinner and he'd have been toast. She'd have dumped him like a bad habit for the hot new partner with the Porsche and the Greenwich split level, leaving Lionel a haggard bachelor drowning his sorrows at one of those dreary Upper East Side pubs.

"Li? Before tomorrow, please?"

He fastened her clasp, and then wrapped his arms around her waist. He kissed her on the neck and entertained a dirty thought. She twisted away and danced off back to the bedroom. He sighed. He always felt like a stuffed boar's head over the mantelpiece when they entertained Lucy's flock. Dan was the only one he felt any true simpatico with, and that was mainly out of a sense of loyalty. Lucy insisted that she and

Dan had never been more than pals, though it would not have surprised Lionel had they enjoyed a shag or two in their college days. It had only taken him about twelve years to let that one go.

Lucy returned to the study in her heels. She spun around theatrically, revealing a simple Maubouissin bauble – a lone ruby on a sterling chain – that dangled a hair's breadth above her cleavage, peeking out from a provocative scoop neck.

"Okay?" she asked with a hopeful smile.

"Breathtaking. You get more beautiful every day."

"Thank you, dear." She examined the polish on one of her nails. She'd just had them done yesterday. Was there already a chip?

"I don't deserve you."

"Oh sweetheart, are you feeling anxious?" Lucy said, ignoring him. She held her hand under the banker's lamp on the piano. No chip. It was just a reflection on the lacquer.

"Not at all."

"Good. My friends are so fond of you. You have nothing to be nervous about."

"I feel like a lap dog."

"Stop it." She tapped out a few notes at his piano. "You can play for Nicole's new beau. It'll be painless, I promise."

"Why me?" Lionel asked helplessly.

"Why you what?"

"Why does a washed-up old fool like me get one moment of your sweet loveliness, much less all of this?" he asked, spreading his arms about their apartment.

"Because as fools go, you are the best."

The intercom buzzed. She stood on tippy toe and kissed him on the nose. "Honey? We've got company!"

- 16 -
CHUCK JAMMED UP

They rode in silence. Except for the deafening howl consuming Chuck's brain as he sat steaming in traffic on the New Jersey Turnpike. The bottleneck had started where the Garden State Parkway merged into eight lanes of hell stretching past the steel towers, burning smokestacks, and wretched stench of petroleum products bubbling out of the industrial maze. They had not moved in twenty minutes. He glanced out the window at the runway at Newark Airport that bordered the highway. The line of planes waiting for takeoff was moving faster than they were. Good thing Paula had insisted they allow plenty of time. At this rate they'd be lucky to get through the Lincoln Tunnel by dessert.

"I assume I'll be driving home tonight," Paula asked. It was more of a statement than a question.

"I might enjoy a beverage or two while you girls are catching up. You can bet Lionel is stocking his usual top-drawer selection."

"Great. So you can move your private bar from Chuck's Tavern to Lucy's living room?"

Chuck decided to table the sour riposte on the tip of his tongue. Paula had endured a lot. And best he could tell, she was not keeping a running bottle count on his inordinate consumption since the plunge began. Small blessing. If she knew the real tally. The car lurched to a stop again. Maybe a plane had missed the runway and crash-landed on the Turnpike. That would explain the monumental tie-up.

"I'll try to be on good behavior," he said.

"I'd appreciate it." Paula sighed and stared straight ahead.

Chuck knew he was being unreasonable. Paula had been urging him to get out more. Play some golf, take up gardening, build a gazebo in their back yard. Anything. How could he explain that he'd rather lie in bed with the shades drawn until cocktail hour than find something productive to do in the middle of a workday afternoon.

Chuck had not been unemployed since college. One thing had led to another, few risks were taken, and the rewards were ample and fairly earned. Somewhere in the back of his mind there were regrets. He had once longed to be in sports management, and he'd even taken some grad-level courses during his senior year towards that goal. Perhaps he'd become a scout for the Yankees. Or general manager of his beloved New York Giants. Sure. Who didn't want that job? There was only one problem. He wasn't prepared to start his climb up the tall mountain of professional athletics as an assistant to the women's basketball coach at Fargo State for 12K a year. Instead, he followed his instincts to go where the more lucrative work was. He had a knack for the wiles of the new software era and moved easily into sales with a major technology concern. In no time at all, he was manager level at a Wall Street firm, running their IT acquisitions department. The fit was perfect. He had a good mind for the vast sprawling enterprise systems, and Wall Street was ramping up so fast that a high school kid could have made a living at what he did. Chuck was a people person with an engaging smile and an easygoing demeanor. Before long, he was nurturing multimillion-dollar relationships with top vendors and found himself entertaining clients in third row seats behind the plate at Yankee Stadium. In a fashion, he had ended up in sports management anyway.

He never saw the crash coming. None of them did. One day business was slow. The next, grown men in shorts and ball caps were hauling Staples boxes out of their downtown offices. Chuck found himself out on the street with two weeks pay and nothing to sell. The prospects were daunting. And that was nine months ago. In no time at all he went from methodical job hunt to panic to resignation. When Paula suggested he join a networking group, he had cringed. Network *what*, he thought.

"What are you doing?" Paula asked, jarring him back to the real world.

The jam-up had finally broken and they'd made it to the Upper East Side, but street parking was proving, as usual, futile. Chuck had the car stopped halfway on the sidewalk, blocking pedestrian traffic, as he strained to read the hourly charges on the sign at the entrance to a Kinney Parking Garage.

"Chuck! People are trying to get by."

"Do you see what they're getting here?" he said, ignoring her. His eyeglass prescription was at least a year behind, but he could still decipher the obscene prices. "Thirty-eight bucks," he seethed. "I should get into the parking business."

You should get into the toll-taking business on the Garden State Parkway if it will improve your mood, Paula thought. A sentiment best left unsaid. Chuck gunned the car back into traffic.

"How about you drop me," she offered in a kinder voice. Maybe a little mercy was in order.

"I suggested that twenty minutes ago."

"I didn't want to abandon you."

"I can manage my abandonment issues."

They pulled up to the elegant brick edifice on East 79th Street. Chuck double-parked as Paula fished her purse out from the back seat. "Shoot. We didn't even bring anything," she said.

"I thought you were going to re-gift that god awful vase the PTA gave you for hosting the bake sale luncheon."

"Why would I give Lucy a vase I hate?"

"Ya got me. Seemed like a plan."

If social graces were left to men, Paula thought. Someone in a SUV honked behind them.

"You don't own enough of the goddamned road already?" Chuck cursed, spinning his head around angrily.

"Chuck, sweetheart. Please?"

He took a deep breath. He really needed to get a grip. "Okay, I'll meet you up there if I'm not circling until midnight."

"Will you give up and garage park it. Just this once. For me?"

"One more lap."

"Just one. Promise?"

"Word of honor."

Paula leaned over and kissed him hard on the mouth, taking the fizz right out of his fight. "I love you."

"Love you too."

"Hey," she said, leaning back into the car. "Can you grab some flowers at the corner store?"

"Sure. No problem."

He watched Paula walk up to the entrance of the building and disappear inside the lobby. He shifted into drive and navigated his way crosstown, making the lights all the way to First Avenue. He swung a right, and then another right onto 78th Street. Now he was in the land of the boxy highrises, fully residential. Surely there would be a space.

No luck. He wound his way back to Madison and gave up. He pulled into a garage by Lenox Hill Hospital. $32.90 for anything over two hours up until six a.m. One step short of extortion and come to think of it, the joint was probably run by the mob. *Well, there goes the scotch budget for the week*, he thought as he handed over the keys to the attendant. Lucy better have made a killer spread.

He walked up Lexington Avenue until he came to a corner store, its sidewalk crammed with flowers. He scoured the selection like a bee circling a field, until he settled on a dozen tulips tinged in mustard yellow and peach. A bit tacky, but they looked fresh enough and besides, at $6.99, he couldn't beat the price. As he watched the Korean clerk wrap the flowers in a sheet of paper, he imagined all the hands his measly bouquet touched on their journey. From some field in Holland, they had to go to the middle-man in Amsterdam, to a hangar at JFK, to another middle-man somewhere in Queens, and finally, onto the back of a cargo van supplying corner stores and bodegas from the Upper East Side to Harlem. It was a wonder anyone made a penny on the deal.

"The Birnbaum/Kaminsky's," he announced to the doorman a moment later, flowers in hand.

"Yes, of course. 12-B. Go right in." The doorman called up ahead of him.

What a throwback, Chuck thought as he admired the murals in the spacious lobby. A protected enclave from another era. The elevator operator looked like he'd been chosen from Central Casting. He manually closed the metallic gates of the outside door and then levered the shift to throw the elevator into its upward journey.

"12-B," Chuck said.

"Yes sir."

They rode in silence until the operator pulled the doors open with a practiced sweep and a clang. "To the left, sir."

"Thanks."

It had been several years. Chuck walked down the unfamiliar hallway until he found the apartment. The door was partially ajar. He rapped with his knuckles three times hard. Nothing. He heard a ruckus coming from inside. What the hell. He let himself in. He was greeted by the sight of his wife doubled over with laughter, tears streaming down her face.

"Hi honey," she said, gasping to catch her breath.

"Good lord, how long was I gone?" he asked, looking curiously at Paula, who still could not speak.

"Oh Chuck," Lucy said, kissing him on the cheek. "How dare you hold her hostage for another moment in New Jersey." She smelled of champagne and Chanel.

He handed her the flowers. "For you. And Lionel of course. He is joining us, isn't he?" He shifted from one foot to the other.

"Good thing you're here, man," a voice boomed out from the kitchen. "I was starting to feel like the odd man out."

Lucy and Paula burst into another peal of laughter as Chuck and Lionel exchanged a perfunctory handshake.

"I think we might just be accessories," Chuck said.

"I'm prepared for that. Offer you champagne, or a real drink?"

"Real sounds good."

Lionel led him through the maze of the apartment to the study, where a wet bar was set up with more bottles than a neighborhood pub.

"What's your poison?" Lionel asked.

"Is that Lagavulin?"

"Sixteen year." He popped the cork and inhaled deeply. "Aye, I can smell the peaty waters of me youth," he said in his best Scottish brogue.

"I shouldn't be hitting your good stuff."

"Not alone you shouldn't," Lionel said, filling two heavy Waterford crystal glasses liberally. "Ice?"

"And ruin a Lagavulin sixteen?"

"Ahhh, a man after my own heart. Cheers mate."

"Cheers to ya."

Chuck inhaled the first sip of the smoky amber fluid. The evening was looking up already.

- 17 -
IN DAN'S HEAD

Hasid on the downtown Number 1 Train. Red line on a Saturday night. Spanish girl, charcoal eyes, great tits. Banker type, pretty woman on his arm. Why no rock on her ring finger? Manhattan teenagers, amazing bodies – tattoos! – carry it so well, like nowhere else. Two black kids hawking candy out of ripped-open cardboard boxes. "We ain't supporting no school or church. We supporting our pockets." At 86th Street station, Psycho Electric Violin Guy – a dead ringer for the guitarist from Scorpion – entertaining the troops with his brand of classical interpretation set to '80s headbanger ball. Chinese man enroute downtown, night shift as the Mott Street dishwasher. Black woman with red hair reading Tolstoy through her Dolce & Gabbana shades. So many young women in scuffed cowboy boots, the subway looks like a rodeo. Tourist family, Salt Lake perhaps? Dad with man purse (is there anything more humiliating?), bored kids with too-white Nikes. Mom with tucked-in tennis shirt. Thinks she is fashion-conscious. Could not be less so.

"What kind of wine did you get?"

"Huhhh?" Dan was in the habit of working on new material for his one-act whenever he rode the subway. He disappeared so deeply into his own head that he sometimes came up three stops past his destination. He even carried a small, lined Clairefontaine notebook and pen in his back pocket. You never knew when inspiration might strike.

"Ahh, some French thing. A red. It'll be fine." He didn't bother to mention that it set them back forty-five bucks. Too much information.

Nora wore a cottony fall skirt with a V-neck sweater, draped with a well-worn jean jacket. It was not too late in the season for flip-flops. Dan loved the thin gold band she wore on the middle toe of her left foot. He enjoyed the sexy image of his wife interviewing the CEO of some godless corporation, hiding the symbol of her rebellion beneath her black Nine West pump.

It was no secret. Dan worshipped Nora. He was insanely proud of her role as a top business journalist. When her *Vanity Fair* piece came out, he dropped a hundred bucks to have the article framed. His wife's name in bold letters in New York's hottest rag. The Writer and The Actor. That was how he viewed them. While he pursued his craft, she brought home the paycheck. When she was wiped out, he played chef. She carried the insurance. He scored the tickets to the Tribeca Film Festival. It was a good arrangement. Good for Nora, good for Dan. He was a lucky goddamned guy.

Dan held her hand as they rode up in the elevator. He savored the reassuring feel of her wedding ring as he spun it between his fingers. Lucy was no doubt applying the finishing touches to what promised to be a delectable repast. Dan loved Lucy too, and Nora's friendship with her meant the world to him. He might not have even married Nora if Lucy had disapproved. It was that actor thing. He was constantly on stage, in search of the glowing review. His shrink said his parents had probably abandoned him emotionally around the age of two – about the time they began recognizing that his older brother's I.Q. was one step short of Einstein's. Rob had Harvard written across his face about the age most boys were learning to crib copies of *Playboy*. No surprise, his life-path delivered the perfect job, the perfect wife, the perfect kids, all in a timely fashion. Dan held no ill will toward his big brother, but it was a tough act to follow. As a result, he was always seeking approval. Lucy's was unconditional. And fortunately, Lucy loved Nora. It was a self-adulation gravy train. He'd had a great run that morning. He'd gotten laid. He even had a good idea for a new character riff in his play. The night was fat with promise.

"Ohmigod, you look amazing!" Lucy welcomed Nora into the flat with a full body hug.

"And what am I, chopped livuh?"

"Yeah, yeah, yeah, Dan. Always the middle child. You need some attention?" Lucy planted a wet kiss smack on his lips. She always did. Nora did not blink. Lucy was not into air kissing. She said that didn't count.

"Dan."

"Lionel." My god the British could be stuffy, Dan thought. They shook hands gravely after Lionel had untangled from his hug with Nora.

"Daniel Danny Dan!" Paula waltzed out of nowhere carrying a champagne-filled flute.

"Heyyy, sweetheart. You look amazing." He tried to mask his lie. Had it been that long? It was not that she looked bad, just – domesticated? Maybe it was New Jersey. Something in the air added a thin sheen of gloss over the wrinkles, like growing grass to keep the weeds at bay. "Where's Chuckles?"

Chuck wandered out from the study with his tankard of whisky. "Hey Dan. Nora," he intoned with all the enthusiasm of a claims adjuster.

Holy shit, Dan thought. Chuck looked like Jake LaMotta in the third reel. He had paunched out at a good two hundred pounds and it was clear that he had bought a belt several sizes too big to hide it. The leather flap corkscrewed from his waist like a drunken ferret. His tennis shirt strained beneath his blazer and his eyes were rimmed and bloodshot.

"Nice to see you, man," Dan said. "You look fortified. Whatcha drinking?"

"Lionel's pouring the good stuff."

"Well, what are we waiting for?"

And with that, in the grand tradition of dinner parties since the beginning of time, the men retired to the study and the women clattered into the kitchen.

- 18 -
NICOLE AND GRAY

Ahhh New York. It still grabbed Nicole every time she came out of the din of Penn Station and onto Seventh Avenue. The billboards pulsed neon. The street was a river of humanity. A line of taxis stretched before them. Nicole felt alive. "C'mon," she said, pulling Gray's hand. "We're late." She had two fingers in the air before he could even catch his breath.

Her bubbly mood amplified as their taxi shot across the Park. She and Lucy had been roommates in the city for only eighteen months, back in the mid-1980s, right after college. But it had been their wonder years, drinking in the marvels of New York with reckless abandon. They shared rent and double dates, summer sublets and even the occasional hapless faux-boyfriend. There was no Internet and people actually hung out and smoked cigarettes and went dancing at dive bars and ate ethnic food on the dangerous Lower East Side. Lucy was slaving away at a single-digit salaried job in a sub-basement NGO, headquartered at the United Nations. Nicole was writing copy for *American Lawyer*, a Saltine-dry trade rag and sure-fire hire for every young wannabe journalist in the city. She and Lucy did not have a dime in the world. They could not have been happier.

"You're going to love Lucy," Nicole babbled to Gray.

"Good title for a show," he smiled. He had been riding coattail to Nicole's enthusiasm ever since the train pulled out of Washington. Expectation was beginning to take its toll.

"Oh honey, I'm sorry. Am I being insufferable?"

"In the most endearing fashion." He kissed her forehead as the taxi idled at a light.

She kissed him on the lips in return. The cab lurched forward, throwing them back hard against the seat, laughing. A moment later they alighted in front of the building.

"Your friends live in style," Gray observed, as Nicole's heels clicked across the marble floor of the lobby.

"Luce is the most down to earth person you will ever meet. Dyed-in-the-wool liberal, born on the wrong side of the tracks in Westchester."

"I didn't know they had a wrong side of the tracks in Westchester."

"Don't be a poop, Gray." She shot him a fake pout. "And don't be fooled by the trappings. Lionel can be a bit of a snob, but that's to be expected. He is a Brit, you know."

"Bad teeth, tea and jam? The sun never sets on the British empire, that whole bloody routine?"

"Something like that. You'll see." She stopped in front of the doorman.

"The Kaminsky/Birnbaums. 12-B. But please don't call up? I want to surprise them. They're expecting us."

"Of course. Several guests are there already. Elevator to the left."

Nicole could barely contain herself, bouncing up and down on her Jimmy Choos as the gates opened on twelve with a metallic swoosh. She hurried down the hall with Gray in tow. They rang the bell and stood in front of the apartment. Laughter wafted out from behind the heavy door. Nicole rang a second time. A voice called from the elevator.

"Ma'am? I believe you lost an earring?" The elevator operator held the gate open.

Nicole reached for her ear. "Oh my lord, yes. Thank you." She pranced back to fetch it.

Gray waited ill at ease, alone. The eyepiece on the locked door clinked as someone peeked out. The deadbolt was unsnapped. The door opened a crack through the secured chain. Lionel gazed suspiciously at Gray. "May I help you?" Lucy appeared through the slender opening behind Lionel, drink in hand.

"Who is it?" she called out with mirthful glee. She peered over Lionel's shoulder. Her smile faded.

"Oh," she said taking Gray in. "The doorman didn't call up about you. Can we help?"

Unexpected guests were about as welcome as vermin in these climes. She and Lionel stared out from behind the chained door into the hallway, at an impasse. Gray stood rock still, caught like a deer in the headlights.

"Luu-cee Kaminkseeeee!"

Nicole's face appeared through the crack, gaily clipping her earring back on.

Lucy clapped her hand to her mouth. Lionel's mouth formed a silent *uh-oh*. Gray turned a steely eye to Nicole. She shrugged. It had never crossed her mind to mention that Gray was black.

Part Two
Soirée

- 19 -
COCKTAIL HOUR

Lucy cleared space amidst the collection of glasses on the coffee table to set down a tray of piping hot Thai crab cakes, each one nestled in a single crisp finger of endive. On the sideboard, an assortment of cheeses and charcuterie rested: spicy sopressata and paper thin Prosciutto de Parma, a wedge of Humboldt Fog and a creamy Brillat-Savarin. Several crunchy Amy's baguettes filled a long concave wooden boat platter that Lionel had picked up during a tour of Portugal. Lucy had ripped a sampling of thumb-sized hunks of fresh bread off in advance to send a signal that this was best. She liked the way the crust broke in her hand and she favored a more primitive style of entertaining than her mother, who would have presented a Georg Jensen sterling silver knife to accompany each individual cheese, set on a 50s-style ceramic plate.

"Ohhh fabulous Luce," Nicole gushed, a speck of breadcrumb affixed to her chin as she devoured a crab cake appetizer. "I'm going to eat the whole platter."

"Thanks sweetie." Lucy plucked her stem glass from the congestion of the coffee table and stepped back to survey the activity. Dan and Paula were going at it like long lost high school friends. Chuck was clutching his drink and gazing out the window onto 79th Street as if he were waiting for a bus. Lionel was nowhere to be seen. Come to think of it, neither was Nora.

Gray sat alone at the edge of the long leather couch. Lucy studied him from afar. He wore crisply pressed slacks and a jet-black wool mock turtleneck. His legs were crossed and she noted his wine colored loafers. His skin was dark, a rich unblemished shade of luxurious chocolate. But what captured her most was his head covering, for he wore what she could only guess was a fez. It was decoratively embroidered with a beaded design that to her eye looked like an African yarmulke.

She was still reeling from the shame of hers and Lionel's horrendous faux pas. Part of her wanted to kill Nicole, but then why should any guest have to announce that their new beau was black. Were she and Lionel to make an appearance at a stranger's home, was it on her to announce that she was arriving with a severely depressed, creatively blocked British conductor with a penchant for whisky and self-loathing? She was grateful that Nic and Gray did not turn around and go straight back to Washington. They would have been in the right for her inexcusable behavior.

She had already tried to gloss over the awkwardness several times, but it was apparent that Gray felt about as welcome as a teetotaler at a wine tasting. She had been planning this evening for weeks. Now the guest of honor was sitting miserably by himself, standing out like a sore thumb. That simply would not do.

She cut her way through the tangle of legs and bodies between the coffee table and the couch and plunked herself down right next to Gray.

"So, we've certainly come a long way with integration, haven't we?" she said brightly.

Gray stared at her like she was wearing a white hood.

"He can be a bit humorless when it comes to the black thing," Nicole said, joining them as she popped another crab cake in her mouth.

"Yes, something about that 200 years of slavery always makes *the black thing* feel a bit close to the bone for me," he replied.

Lucy perked up. He spoke. It was a start. "Nicole tells me you're a cultural anthropologist."

She smiled at Gray with the patience of someone who planned to sit there until daybreak if need be. He studied her with his head cocked, like she was some kind of rare bird. A parrot perhaps.

"That is an august word for it," he replied. "I am a professor."

"At Georgetown."

"Correct."

Their conversation was just crackling along. Not to be put off, Lucy put her hand very gently to his scalp. "I love your fez."

Gray looked at Lucy, unsure of what to make of this Jewish woman patting him on the head like a dog. "It's a kufi," he said at last.

He was seething inside. It just goes to show, he thought. Forty years of domestic apartheid, you rise above it all to earn two Masters and a Ph.D. – and you still get mistaken for a house robber. Part of him wanted to walk out the door even as Nicole led him in. He could think of better ways to spend an evening than hanging out with a bunch of apologetic, New York, left-wing reactionaries. That was strong brew, one you needed to have a taste for. But Nicole had a way of cooling him off, even at his most defiant. And the evening was all about Nicole. He had volunteered for this service. And besides, truth be known, he had worn the kufi on purpose. His intentions could not have been more premeditated. How many times had Angela accused him of putting on his defensive black man pose before a punch had even been thrown? That was the problem when your third wife held an esteemed Chair in the sociology department at American University, and was even darker-skinned than you. There was little opportunity to play the race card.

Oh well. He supposed he better give these white people a chance. Nicole hadn't known him long enough to see his Hate Whitie side. Tonight was probably not the best time to let it out of the bag. He tried to relax the tension in his jaw as he reached for a bite of crab.

"What is a kufi?" Lucy asked.

"It's North African. It's often mistaken for a fez. Men wore it to tribal ceremonies."

"You're from North Africa?"

"My relatives were." He was subconsciously backing off already. At least he didn't say *ancestors*. He needed to know his audience better before he went down that road. "The crab is very good."

"Gray can't boil an egg," Nicole announced. She planted a kiss on his cheek. "The man's raised three kids, lived alone for years, and his idea of haute cuisine is a microwaved Wolfgang Puck pizza."

What a beautiful couple, Lucy thought. She felt her Jewish liberalism kicking in, even as she fought to gaze at them without blinders. Gray was the blackest black man she had ever met. Not like the pale-skinned garden variety Negroes she vaguely knew at Brown, and then later, at the law firm. Gray was the real deal. She was still unnerved by hers and Lionel's reaction at the door. Was it truly fear, or just their barely masked class-consciousness that made them react so?

Gray was about as threatening as an insurance salesman. Would they have flinched if this well-dressed stranger was as pale as a bed sheet?

"What do you teach, old man?"

Gray spun around. Lionel appeared as if on cue, entrance stage right. His voice boomed with stentorian authority. His drink, Lucy noted, was filled to the brim.

"Contemporary African Politics in a Global Geo-Conscious Environment."

"Translation?"

"How do we get out from under white man's rule."

Chuck looked up from the window. This had potential. He meandered back into the sunken living room.

"Interesting," Nora said, drifting in from out of nowhere. "I'd love to see the course syllabus. Are you teaching undergraduate level?"

It was as if the whole room had suddenly been given permission to talk to the black guy, Gray thought.

"Yes. It's the last chance to get them," he said.

"Get who?" Lucy asked.

"The minds of the young. The disenfranchised black male in particular. Though sadly, most of the ones who end up at Georgetown haven't been told they're disenfranchised." Gray popped a jalapeno-stuffed olive in his mouth.

Lucy offered up a cocktail napkin. "What do you mean?"

"My class list ends up being the cream of the crop. The lawyers to be. The doctors, the investment bankers. They show up to hear the fireworks, the histrionics, the black-man-must-rise-above-it-all jargon. Then they go on to get their degrees and their Wall Street jobs and their six-figure bonuses and their house in the 'burbs. The kids I teach don't end up becoming civil rights leaders marching in Selma. You're not going to find them standing atop an Olympic podium in

Mexico City with a black glove raised in protest."

"Honey? No one's climbing any podiums with black gloves raised any more," Nicole said sweetly.

Gray glared at her. Wasn't she supposed to be on his side?

"God knows your work is brilliant," she soothed, reading his mind. "You know I feel that way. But you're teaching history, not activism. The black experience has changed since you were younger. What the kids know today is Jay-Z and Kanye and Nas. Not Malcolm X."

"Yes dear, I'm aware of that," Gray said, attempting to keep his river of irony to a mere drip. "That's the problem. You and I, and your lovely well-appointed friends, we all ride up in a gilded elevator to this aerie high above the Upper East Side, where we can look down in judgment. We're the privileged few, the plantation owners, the ruling class. We're perpetually on our way up. But do you know why so many people are dialed in about this particular recession? It's not just about class differences any more – the one-percent and all that hype. It's because the white American male has *become* the class difference. He's feeling the pinch. The easy refis have disappeared. Mom and Dad can't afford to send the kids to their alma mater. The country club membership is gone. 'No new BMW this year, Punkin'. We really need to reel it in a bit.'"

"Not everyone in this room is driving around in a gleaming white BMW," Paula said quietly. She stared down at her hands, clasped in her lap. Chuck looked at his wife with surprise. Public proclamations were usually not her thing.

Gray studied Paula, preparing to pounce. Then he remembered: he was a guest at this party. He trained his safe lecture face on her.

"I am aware that the class rifts in America have grown in

disparity," he said, momentarily backpedaling. "But the young African male isn't even in the demographic mix. How does an 18-year-old black high school dropout define a recession?"

"Maybe dropping out is the first problem," Paula said, growing bolder. Everyone was treating Nicole's date like Martin Luther King himself had descended from the Pearly Gates. Granted, the sight of a black man walking down the street in her cozy little New Jersey hamlet usually resulted in a call to 9-1-1. But did that mean she had to kowtow to his eminence?

Gray glowered at Paula, barely able to contain himself. Good thing Nicole didn't warn him about this little housewife number from the sticks. He might not have bothered to come.

"You don't understand, do you," he said. "None of you do. If a young black urban male is not in jail – and let's face it, the statistics say there's a darned good chance of him paying a visit at some point – then he's unemployed, and more than likely living in a single-parent household. He can't read at the high school level. He can't write well enough to fill out a job application. There are probably drugs in the mix. Maybe an out-of-wedlock child. Where's his road out? He was born down. And he is stuck there. It hasn't changed since the first slave boat made landfall." Gray adjusted his kufi and massaged the bulging vein running from beneath it.

"Is that what you're teaching?" Paula asked.

It's what I'm living, Gray thought. You think people don't judge me by the color of my skin, just because I have a chair in the history department at Georgetown? Hell, you all did. God knows why I expected anything different. It's the same everywhere. Who's the black dude with the great-looking white chick? White people just don't get it. You're so goddamned uptight around a black man that your voice actually changes when you talk to us. You put on a fake smile. Do you think we don't notice? At least Mr. Hotshit conductor seems honest. I'm surprised he didn't slam the door in my face when we first arrived. He was thinking about it. But his wife, she's straight out of the Brandeis playbook. "Some of my best friends are black."

He tried to rope it in. "I teach pride in culture. I teach self-sufficiency. I teach permission to question. I teach young black men that they don't have to 'Be Like Mike.' Remember that uplifting little Madison Avenue epithet?"

"Sounds like you teach indignation," Chuck said.

"Someone's got to," Dan chimed in. Nora looked up from her iPhone, which she had been quietly checking as the conversation raged on.

"I mean, the guy's right," Dan continued. "Who do we expect young black men to model? Michael Vick?"

"Perfect," said Lionel. "A towering monument to athletic grace, black pride, and sheer stupidity."

Oy, how did we get here, Lucy thought. The roast hadn't even come out of the oven yet.

"Do you think," Gray said to Lionel, "that the law should have looked the other way for Vick? Do you think there'd be a new arena in Brooklyn if Jay-Z wasn't singing about the hood, and black athletes weren't modeling crime and gangsta as the hippest thing since Earth, Wind and Fire?"

"You know what I think?" Lionel said, stirring the ice thoughtfully in his drink with one finger. "I think there's not a snowball's chance in hell that a bunch of white folks like us can tell a distinguished African American professor how one should feel about the black experience in America. But you know what I'd really like to know?" His gaze zeroed in north of Gray's eyebrow. "Where can I get a funky-ass skullcap like that thing you're wearing on your head?"

The room fell silent as a golf match. Gray peered at the collection of strangers. At his Georgetown lectern, he was the rock star. Here, he was just another working stiff in a navy Brooks Brothers blazer. He always liked that about New York. It was a good town to be black, educated, and anonymous. And besides, Nicole was watching him like a hawk. He was hardly in the mood to be hightailing it alone back to his empty D.C. apartment on the late-night Amtrak.

He rose from the couch and removed the kufi, revealing a distinguished patch of short, curly gray hair. He held out the head covering with both hands, like an offering to the gods. Lionel accepted it with a generous bow of thanks.

"What *I'd* really like to know, Maestro," Gray asked in an equally somber tone, "is have you written anything worth a good goddamned since that insufferable movie ditty of yours?"

Nicole rolled her eyes as Lucy held her breath. Dan could barely contain himself. Even Chuck looked concerned. Then Lionel let out a belly laugh like Santa Claus. "C'mon Professor. I'll show you my study."

* * *

Lucy sliced and quartered the last of the fresh brussel sprouts, shaved from the long gnarly stalks that she had purchased at the Greenmarket. Something about those stalks – they were so of the earth – made her feel like Alice Waters in a French country kitchen. Were she only able to sneak out the back door and find herself in Provence, snipping a few twigs of lavender and sage. Oh well.

She had cooked up a half pound of bacon earlier in the day, so that the whole apartment didn't reek of bacon grease. She fetched the thick salty cuts from the fridge and started chopping them into meaty little bits. The pine nuts were already toasting on the Viking six-burner stove, a luxury that she cherished despite the fact it set them back nearly the cost of a small car. She was doing a fast sauté for the evening's vegetable. Back in the dark ages, her mother had boiled brussel sprouts to within an inch of their life, leaving a nutrition-free dish that tasted like stale sweat socks. Lucy had refined the recipe, livening it up with diced carrots and garlic and flavored with the bacon. It never failed to shock her guests that brussel sprouts could taste so darned good.

Lionel's pie sat cooling on the counter. She gently slid his masterpiece off to the side and shuffled a cutting board full of quartered sprouts into her sizzling wok. She felt two hands from behind clasp her around her waist, nearly grazing her breasts.

"Dan?"

"Shit. How did you know?"

"Well for starters, you don't smell like Old Spice and expensive whisky."

"If I had, would you have chosen me?"

"Doubtful." She removed his hands and scooped up another mound of vegetables. "Sex life been a bit on the slow side, honey?" She dumped the veggies into the wok.

"Actually, I got laid about an hour ago."

"Ughhh. Too much information." Lucy handed Dan her nine-inch Wusthof. "Here. Make yourself useful."

"Anything for you."

"Chop the rest of those carrots?"

"*Avec plaisir.*"

"Eighth-inch squares, *s'il vous plait.* I need them brunoised."

"Yes, Julia Child." Dan was used to Lucy's demands in the kitchen. They'd been doing this going on twenty years. They were like a married couple, only with all the good parts and none of the baggage.

"How's life, Luce?" he asked, squeezing out a small space next to her at the long counter and tucking into the stack of carrots.

"Not bad."

"Hardly a rave review."

"Well, you know."

"Lionel still auditioning for the role of Grumpy?"

"Don't be mean."

"Coulda had me. Then you'd be living with Dopey."

"Stop trying to cheer me up," she said, trying to suppress a smile.

"What did the bartender say to the horse sitting at the bar?"

"Why the long face," they said in unison, laughing. They had their routine down to a science.

"How's this?" Dan asked, showing her his cutting board expertise.

"If the acting doesn't fly, they'll take you on the line at Le Bernardin in a heartbeat." She scraped Dan's brunoise into the wok, the crisp orange carrot dice adding to the sizzling sauté.

"So?" Dan asked, raising his eyebrows knowingly at Lucy. Dan and Lucy had stood up for one another at their respective weddings. Lucy was the only friend who came to Chicago to see his play. Dan played the role of Godfather to the baby Isaac, handing him off to the mohel at the bris. Lucy could more readily hide from the IRS than keep anything from Dan.

"I visited my Mom today," she said, deflecting him from her more pressing subterfuge. Even Dan wasn't privy to her Harlem excursions. She had considered letting him in, but then she ran the risk of ending up in his one-act play. Some things were best left unsaid.

"Well, there you go. Feeling especially masochistic today, are we?"

"Be nice. She's my mother."

"She *was* your mother. The shell of a human being who lives in that depressing castle on York has nothing to do with the woman who used to make us fabulous Thanksgiving dinners when I couldn't get back to California during college."

"She was a good cook," Lucy smiled softly.

"Her daughter inherited the gene."

"I miss her."

"I know you do."

"Do you think I'm becoming her?"

"Oh my God, Lucy. What did they put in your drink?"

"Whatever it is, it wasn't enough." She swept one last board of brussel sprouts into the wok and reached for the Sancerre she had been working on. It was nearly drained. Jeez, she thought. Lionel and I are both going to end up at Betty Ford. All the same, the crisp white splashed merrily into her goblet.

"But enough about me," Lucy said, changing the subject. "How are you?"

"I'm good, actually."

"You sound surprised."

"Well, besides being flat broke, unable to land work, and wondering if this new agent of mine is worth the card stock I printed my headshots on, I'm getting somewhere with the one-act."

"Great," Lucy said with real enthusiasm. At least one of the men in her life was able to fill a page.

"And Nora? Previous X-rated activities aside, how is she?"

"My brilliant, provocative, sexy journalista? She's

fabulous. Couldn't be better."

Nora sat on the toilet seat scrolling through her messages with one hand while she wiped herself with the other. Apparently Lucy had wireless pulsing through every inch of the apartment. What a luxury. Strong signal, even in the loo.

Nothing. Her email queue was empty.

Had she lost her mind? She was like a junkie, a CrackBerry-head. A lovelorn teen in search of a crumpled note in her grade school locker. Very mature, Nora. If she was going to submarine her marriage, the least she could do was go out and cheat like a normal person. It wasn't as if the thought hadn't crossed her mind before. Years ago, in a vodka-infused moment of pique, she had kissed a stranger at a downtown loft party. It didn't seem such a big deal. A minor transgression at best. Didn't everyone dabble in infidelity at least once? The host of the trendy do had poured VC money into a dotcom startup that she was covering for a forgettable business rag. She couldn't recall if his dreamchild was about Internet security or software design. She only remembered that he was going to change the world. Starting with her worldview. The kiss had lasted a moment. The VC's company not much longer.

The toilet flushed. She scoured her phone in search of a crumb. Was she totally to blame? Dan was a handful all right. Life With A Thespian. A real seven-ticket ride. Somewhere along the road her luster had dimmed for supporting his habit. The glamour of his next role had been replaced by a deep uneasy sense that something was amiss. Maybe their marriage had lost its way. She wondered if Dan had even noticed that she'd gone back on the Pill.

She heard laughter from the living room. She refreshed her screen one last time. A Match icon popped up. Her heart leapt. She clicked on her inbox. Sighhh. Wrong number. Considering she hadn't even posted a photo, she sure was getting a lot of responses. Maybe a piece for the Modern Love column in The Times? she mused.

She quickly skimmed through the rambling note from BigBoatBigHart. "You write eloquntly," it read. The rest was such hopeless prose that she couldn't even get to the end. What was with these people? Not only was this guy's face about ten years older than his profile boasted, but he could not spell, either. "Eloquntly?" Priceless.

Her Dr. Greg was a poet. His brief missives were tantalizing like haiku, and yet subtle in their delivery. He was threatening in the most non-threatening of ways. He had posted only one picture, but it spoke volumes to her: the tasteful indigo tennis shirt he wore untucked, the sexy patch of hair showing just a peek through the open collar on a very appealing and lean chest. She thought his eyes were beautiful. She wondered what he looked like in person. She wondered if she would ever hear from him again.

* * *

"I could kill you," Lucy said, pouting her lips and reapplying a gentle kiss of cranberry gloss.

Nicole's eyebrows skewered upward like two innocent question marks, her delicate features reflected alongside Lucy's in the bedroom vanity mirror. "*Moi? Pourquoi?*"

"How could you not tell me?"

"Tell you what?" Nicole applied her own shade of lipstick to her innocent smirk.

"I thought I was going to die."

"Yes. You of all people. I never would have pegged you as the Upper East Side bitch who slams the door in the black guy's face."

Lucy gaped at Nicole. Nicole's arrow straight expression cracked an inch. Lucy enveloped her in her arms. "Oh have I missed you."

"You too, sweetie."

The two women came unclenched.

"He's beautiful, Nic. And he's brilliant and academic and pretentious, and he's got that Henry Louis Gates meets Jon Stewart thing going on. God I could just stare at him all night long."

"Thanks honey. I knew you guys would hit it off."

"Are you, uhhh, like thinking about getting, married?"

Nicole raised a hand. "*Quel horreur.* The ink hasn't even dried on my divorce papers yet."

"I know, I know. I'm sorry. You know how it is. We bored empty nesters have to live vicariously through our divorced friends."

"So glad to be of service. And since when are you bored? Has his pontificating lordship run out of new material?"

"He's in a bit of a dry spell." An uncomfortable silence fell over Lucy.

Nicole scrutinized her, studying between the lines. Then her mouth fell open in a perfectly formed *O*. "Oh my God." Nicole took Lucy's hands in hers. "Don't tell me. You haven't. Is there someone else?"

"Me?" Lucy burst out laughing like a madwoman. "Are you kidding? Puh-leeez."

"Don't feed me that poor little rich girl line, sister. You are a picture. You could have any man you want in this town."

"Yes, I know. That's what Lionel tells me. About twenty-three times a day."

"Oh dear. The lion's grown protective?"

"You could say that." Lucy reached into her vanity drawer and got out her mascara. "So. How are Emily and Justin?"

"Lucy?"

"Nicole?"

135

"What are you not telling me?"

The lights were low in the bedroom and Lucy could see her face reflected in the mirror behind Nicole. Something about the scene immersed her in a profound sense of déjà vu. She and Nicole used to imagine what their lives might hold: yachts and diamonds, the red carpet and the glittering gowns – a fairy tale that could only flourish in the minds of teenage girls. Now, observing the two of them silhouetted in their black cocktail dresses, Lucy wondered how they had become so grown up?

"Luce?"

A bell started dinging from the kitchen. Lucy shrugged sweetly. Time for the roast to come out.

* * *

"If the fast-rising British conductor had one moment of doubt on stage, it was not apparent during last night's tour de force. The final movement was proffered with a breezy air, like a warm Tuscan eve. The brisk tempo that Mr. Birnbaum set might have been risky, but he kept his performers limber and fluid, with occasional muscular overtones. His concepts were heady and refreshing, and the audience shared his fervor as he led with barely controlled enthusiasm."

Gray set the framed review back down on the cluttered desk. "Not bad," he mused. "When was this?"

"I believe Thatcher was in office," replied Lionel, noodling at the baby grand. Chuck occupied a space by the windowsill, tinkling the ice cubes in his Waterford tumbler. He knew it was a crime adding ice to Lagavulin, but he figured it was the lesser evil to passing out before dinner.

"So you don't conduct any more?" Gray asked.

"No. I'm not *asked* to conduct any more," Lionel

corrected him.

"Forgive my naiveté," Gray said, "but your world is a country mile from mine. Why have you been blacklisted?"

Lionel smiled at the choice of words. "It's not so much blacklisted, as excluded from the club."

Gray raised an eyebrow inquisitively.

"I was a newcomer in a young man's game when that review came out."

"I thought conductors were supposed to be mature, like a fine wine."

"Yes. The mature ones are. The legends. The Mehtas. The Mazurs. The Mutis."

"Maybe you should change your name to Mazursky."

"Mendelssohn would work," Lionel laughed. He took a hit off his drink. "It was a different era. They were true maestros and composers back then. Brilliant artists who could rest on their laurels. Today, everyone needs pop, sizzle, action. The boards of directors in the major cities want their symphonies to be led by someone who looks good on television. PBS specials put bodies in seats. Seats in venues that cost $100 million to build. It's not enough to be a trained conductor, anymore. You have to not only be able to lead the 1812, but do it on a skateboard in spandex shorts."

"Come on, man. Nicole couldn't stop boasting about you on the ride up. You do put bodies in seats."

"High chairs is more like it." Lionel removed the Grammy from the built-in oak shelf. It had a nice heft to it. He handed it to Gray, who read the inscription and handed the statuette back.

"My kids loved this movie. Though I confess, if I ever heard that goddamned song again—."

"You'd take hostages?"

"Precisely."

"It pays for good whisky." Lionel grabbed the bottle from the bar to top himself off. "Chuck, you good?"

"Helped myself. Thanks though."

"You expecting someone? You've been posted up at that window like a sharpshooter ever since you got here."

"Just enjoying the view from above."

"Knock yourself out, mate." Lionel took another swallow and plunked out the opening keys of Beethoven's 5th for good measure. Gray smiled and chuckled softly to himself.

* * *

"Have you guys ever considered moving back to the city?" Lucy asked, handing Paula the Baccarat water pitcher to carry out to the dining room.

If we could live like this, she thought.

"It hasn't come up. The way things are going, though, we might be moving to a trailer park soon."

"Aww sweetie." Lucy set her stack of salad plates down and squeezed Paula's shoulder with one hand. More like a coach exhorting an athlete than a full-on hug. A reassurance. "Is there anything I can do to help?"

"Know anybody looking for a senior accountant?" Paula asked. "One who's been out of the workforce since espadrilles were in fashion, and is still running Windows 95 on her laptop?"

"No way," Lucy said. "Are you really looking for work?"

"Way."

"Paula. I didn't know it was that bad."

"Trust me. I signed up on LinkedIn. I had to write a resume. Do you know how many Belvedere and grapefruits that took? God, what a sorry document that turned out to be. Don't tell Chuck," she whispered.

"Why?" Lucy asked.

"Are you kidding? He'd freak if he knew. The only thing lower than our savings account is his bruised ego. The last thing he needs to hear is that his wife is thinking of returning to the workforce."

"Since when is that a negative?" Lucy asked.

"Oh boy, you haven't been out to our neck of the woods in a while, have you. Pigs will fly before most of the women I know will admit they're job hunting."

"That's kind of pathetic," Lucy said.

"Tell me about it."

"Is Chuck anywhere near a job offer?"

"I can't even get him near a lawnmower. Frankly, he's driving me a little nuts. I shove him out the door to Subway just to buy five free minutes to myself."

"I hear you," Lucy said. "Don't forget, I live with an at-home artist. I'm no stranger to Puttering Husband Syndrome."

"True," Paula laughed. "We all tend to forget that."

"You mean in the bright light of Sir Lionel's prowess?"

"It's easier to drink in all of this," Paula said, casting her arms theatrically about the apartment, "than to remember that you guys have lives, too."

"This was a third floor walkup not so long ago."

Paula did forget. They all did. Everything came so easily to Lucy. She even seduced the right conductor. Had Paula picked a musician, he probably would have turned out to be a one-hit wonder from Yugoslavia. She'd be raising her kids in a Serbo-Croatian ghetto.

"You guys will get through it," Lucy said, snapping Paula back to planet Earth.

"I sure hope so. The rope's getting awfully frayed."

Nicole and Nora strolled into the kitchen.

"What can I do to help?" Nicole asked.

"Tell us what it's like to have a husband who has a job," said Lucy. "You're the only one here who can report on that particular phenomenon."

"I don't have a husband. I have a boyfriend."

"Well there you go," said Nora. "Key to a successful relationship."

"Cheers to that," Lucy agreed. Glasses were raised and clinked. A timer went off. Lucy opened the oven door to check on her roast.

"Lionel honey," she called out in the direction of the living room. "Time to let the wine breathe."

In no time at all, the troops assembled in the kitchen. Lionel pored over the collection of assembled reds he had placed in a row on the counter top.

"Hope this works," Dan said, holding up his investment like a trophy for Lionel to inspect.

"Thanks," Lionel replied, pushing his glasses to the end of his nose in order to read the small print on the bottle. "Ahhh, very nice. You didn't need to do that."

A cell phone went off.

"Is that mine?" Lucy asked, removing the roasting pan from the oven with a pair of mitts. She set it down to cool on a ceramic trivet.

"Mine," said Paula, taking the call.

Nora surreptitiously checked her messages as Lucy wriggled past and opened the fridge.

"Hang on, honey," Paula said into her phone. "Let me ask your father." Chuck was busy working up a case of kitchen envy, poring over Lucy's Delonghi espresso maker, tucked away in a corner by the pantry.

"Chuck? How do we feel about Missy spending the night with Carla?"

"Is anyone else going to be there?" he replied, looking up from the glistening silver machine.

"Who did you have in mind?" Paula asked.

"A couple of parents, for example?"

"Oh my God, Chuck. You're kidding, right?" Lucy asked.

"Absolutely not," he replied. "Have you seen my daughter, lately? Not to mention her friends. They're a handful of teenage pregnancies waiting to happen." Paula shot him a look that could cut glass.

"You think any chaperone could prevent that?" Lucy said.

"If the chaperone were me, you better believe it," Chuck fired back.

"And I assume you had the same set of rules for Tommy?"

"Hell no. He was a boy." Lucy rolled her eyes as she pulled out a small stainless steel bowl from a cabinet by the sink.

"Honey, talk to your Dad," Paula said, exasperated, handing off the phone. "Here."

Chuck placed it to his ear. "Hey Missy. Watcha doin'?"

Gray, who had been observing from afar, set down his tumbler and rummaged through his pocket until he came up with his Android. Nicole slipped an arm through his. "Two-timing me?" she asked.

"Only with my ex," he replied, checking his texts. "Brianna's home from Northwestern."

"Pretty name," Lucy chimed in. "How many children do you have?"

"Two daughters from my second marriage. And a son from my first."

"Busy, busy. Have you and Nicole introduced the kids to

each other?"

"No!" Gray and Nicole said simultaneously. Nicole stood on tiptoe and planted a loud smooch on Gray's cheek.

"Ahhh, young love," Lucy said with a smile.

Chuck's voice rose over the chatter of conversation. "It's fine by me. As long as somebody's folks are there."

"Like she'd tell you if they weren't," Dan said, eavesdropping. "When my parents left town, all hell broke loose."

"Yes, you were boys," said Nora.

"Boys in pursuit of sex," Lucy added.

"Precisely," said Dan. "Find someone over eighteen to buy the pony keg. Invite a few stoners to provide the weed. Get the word out and bring it on. Hence, girls lying to parents about their whereabouts. I mean wasn't that what high school was all about?"

"Amazing we didn't all get knocked up by tenth grade," Nicole said.

"We pulled out," Dan replied.

"Disgusting," said Lucy. "Can we not discuss semen while I'm making the horseradish sauce?" She scooped a healthy dollop of mayo into the mixing bowl and proceeded to whip it into a froth.

"Okay honey," Chuck said, wrapping up his call. "Love you. Have fun. See you tomorrow." Chuck handed the phone back to his wife.

"So?" Paula asked.

"Carla's parents are home."

"Phewww," Paula said, rolling her eyes in jest.

The mellifluous tones of yet another phone rang. Lucy located her iPhone on the kitchen counter top, next to the pan of sizzling brussel sprouts.

"My God," Lionel said, pulling down a trove of wine

glasses from a high cabinet. "What have we wrought?"

"Twenty-first century Armageddon, dear," Lucy said. "My husband lives in the dinosaur age," she confided to Nora, who was still discreetly checking her email. "I believe he owns the last working flip-phone in New York." Lucy removed the salad bowl from the kitchen clutter and headed out to the dining room, phone pressed between her ear and shoulder.

"Yes, Hi. Is she resting comfortably now?" Lucy asked, listening to the response even as she searched through the sideboard for her good salad implements. "Terrific. Thanks so much for getting back to me." A visit to her mother's home always prompted a flurry of maintenance calls. It usually absolved her guilt for another few weeks, until the impulse next struck. She hit the touchpad to end the call.

"Nic, you want to serve the salad," she said. "I dressed it for everyone."

"Sure."

"I didn't even think to ask. Is Gray allergic to anything?"

"No clue," Nicole said. "But he scarfed down about ten of your crab cakes and he still seems to be breathing, so I guess we're safe."

Nicole put her wine glass down and started distributing the fresh greens on the pretty little Bernardaud salad plates Lucy had set out. Lionel carried several open bottles of red to the sideboard. Ceramic bowls and platters full of food started moving to the dining room. Chuck wandered over to the bookshelf in the corner and examined the elaborate sound system.

"Well, will you look at this," he said. Buried amidst a veritable deejay's collection of tuners and receivers and amplifiers, was a vintage turntable resting on a pull-out shelf. "Lionel, does the record player work?" Chuck asked.

"Like a dream," he said.

Dan stepped over to investigate. "You're showing your age, Chuck."

"I know. And I'm growing man breasts, too. It's very unsettling."

"Thanks for sharing, dear," Paula announced, walking out with the brussel sprouts.

Dan fired up the tuner and receiver. The men knelt down next to Lionel's copious record collection lining the built-in just above the parquet floor.

"Lionel? Where do you keep the good stuff?" Dan asked.

"I've got the original Deutchse Gramophone recording of the Bruch Violin Concerto Number One in the basket under the booster amp. Handle like plutonium. It is extremely rare."

"I was thinking more along the lines of The Doobies."

"The what?"

"My Lionel," Lucy said. "He hasn't listened to anything more recent than Rubber Soul since disco came out. Look under there." She deftly steered the men toward a cabinet with one toe as she set the meat platter down. "That's where I keep *my* collection."

Chuck and Dan began to rummage through the records.

"Mars Hotel?" Chuck said. "That is some vintage Dead."

"Ohhh man," Dan crowed, examining the record. "Lucy and I used to get baked to this in college."

"We don't have to give away all our secrets, do we?" Lucy said.

Chuck unearthed Steely Dan's Pretzel Logic. He slipped the disc out of its jacket and set it on the turntable. He lowered the needle. The opening chords of *Rikki Don't Lose That Number* kicked in.

Lionel walked out of the kitchen wielding a gleaming twelve-inch carving knife and a stone. He started stropping the knife back and forth with a zipping, metallic scratch.

"Are you planning a human sacrifice?" Gray asked.

A cell phone cut Lionel off before he could reply. Everyone started searching about like a scavenger hunt, trying to track down the offending unit. Finally Dan came up with his device.

"Hullo?" He paused and listened. "Heyyy. No way. Really? The one from last weekend? Get the fuck out." Dan noticed that the entire room was hanging on his every word. "Look," he said more subtly into his phone. "Let me call you later, okay? Yeah. Yah. Excellent. Take pictures. Bye." Dan slipped his phone into his blue jeans pocket. Lionel stood poised with the carving knife. Chuck held a bottle of red, awaiting the pour. Lucy and Nicole hung in suspense.

"So?" Nora asked. "Are you going to give it up?"

"You remember my buddy Ira? From the events company?"

"Uh huh."

"He just got laid."

"Wonderful," Nora said.

"What are you, like sixteen Dan?" Lucy asked, laughing.

Dan flashed a thousand-watt smile and held up both hands in feigned innocence. Another phone chirped.

"Dear God almighty," roared Lionel.

"Sweetheart," Lucy admonished. "Please don't have a coronary before dinner."

"Enough!" Lionel stepped from the table, knife still in hand, nearly knocking over several wine glasses in the process.

"What are you doing, Li?" Lucy asked. It was nice to see his moribund spirits revived, but she didn't want to have to replace their whole set of Lalique stems.

Lionel set down his carving implements and tapped on his wine glass with a butter knife.

"Friends, I must beg your indulgence," he announced with great fanfare. "My wife has slaved to prepare you this abundant feast of Brobdingnagian proportions."

"Oh boy," Lucy murmured, whispering to Nicole. "Two sheets to the wind and we haven't even started the first course."

"Last time I saw him this gone, didn't he try to feel me up?"

"Did you have to remind me," Lucy said.

"I will not have her labors sullied by these untoward interruptions." Lionel fetched the wooden Portuguese bread bowl from the sideboard and in one fell swoop, dumped the remains all over the counter top. Several pieces fell to the floor. Lucy heard the crunch as his black suede oxford ground an errant crust into their hand-woven Kashmir rug.

"Ohhh," Lucy sighed. Lionel returned to the dining table. He held out his quarry like a tithing bowl.

"Phones please," Lionel commanded.

"Honey. Can you just carve the roast?" Lucy begged.

"I cannot. Now if you can all place your precious devices in this bowl." He rapped it several times on the table for emphasis. An awkward pause ensued. Lionel gazed sternly at his audience. Nicole flashed a sympathetic glance towards Lucy. She rolled her eyes. Food was growing cold.

"What are you going to do Li, microwave the whole lot of them?"

"A delicious idea dear, but I'm merely offering a graceful proposition." He turned to the group. "May we try to live for one bloody hour without our infernal phones?"

"Forget it," Paula said. "No can do."

"Of course you can," Lionel said.

"No I cannot. You do remember I have children?"

"Yes Paula, dear friend. You are not the first human to procreate. And I am confident your loving progeny will somehow meander through the long perilous night, even if you are not available by text."

"How lyrical," Paula said with a snort. "But I like to know that when my daughter is out gallivanting about the back roads of New Jersey, if she gets a flat tire or runs out of gas, she can reach me."

"Yes, because heaven knows, prior to the cell phone, no one ever had a flat tire. God forbid they had to flag down help or walk to the nearest gas station."

"Oh Lionel, don't be such a cliché," Nora butted in. "Do you want everyone to return to the dark ages? Do you play your music on sticks and cans?"

"It is how music was invented." An audible groan went up from the table.

"Lionel, everyone's hungry," Lucy said. Her patience was wearing thin.

"I concur with Paula," Gray piped in with professorial authority.

"What did I say?" Paula whispered to Lucy.

"Beats me."

"We cannot unburden ourselves of the technological umbilical cord. Try as we may, it's our lifeline." Gray held up his phone as a prop for his dissertation. "Let's face it. It's not just business calls and meaningless texts that keep us tethered. Why do we really clutch these to our breasts? I'll tell you why. Because of the unimaginable and the unexpected. That, is the cell phone's true role in the greater fabric."

"Here we go," Nicole announced.

"The iPhone is the lock and key to our darkest

emotions," Gray continued, ignoring his girlfriend's skeptical stare. "The text from the sitter. Johnnie's fallen down. The infant is choking on a marble. The house is ablaze."

"Honey?" Nicole interrupted to no avail. He was on a roll.

"The late night call with news of the unspeakable." Gray cast a somber gaze about the table. "The last missives from the burning towers. That's what we're really waiting for." His voice faded to silence. No one spoke a word.

"Well," Nicole said brightly. "That's a real pick-me-up."

"How about dinner?" Lucy said. "Maybe afterwards we can enjoy a nice chitchat about the genocide in Syria."

"Bollocks to all of you," Lionel said, picking up the razor sharp carving knife. "I applaud the good professor. Well done, squire." Lionel sliced like a caveman into the quivering meat with good-natured gusto. Paula passed the bowl of brussel sprouts. Chuck grabbed one of the open bottles of red and walked around the table, filling each rose-shaped goblet. The dulcet harmonies of Steely Dan filled the room.

Lucy disappeared into the kitchen. She returned a moment later with a tall vase blooming with the purple irises she had purchased from the Greenmarket. She cleared a spot and placed them for the finishing touch. Lionel found a book of matches and lit the tapered dinner candles with a flourish. He hit the dimmer switch on the nearby wall and lowered the lights. Then he returned to the head of the table. He raised his wine glass and pinged on it with one sharp click of his finger for attention.

"Friends, guests, lovers, companions: a toast. To my precious gem, my effervescent ruby – my Luce," he said, spreading his arms like Jesus across the vast spread. "*C'est fête pour la roi.*"

"I thought the British hated the French," Gray

whispered to Nicole.

"Just run with it," she smiled, taking a sip. Then she raised her glass, too. "Everybody? To Lucy. Bon appetit!"

- 20 -
MAIN COURSE

Cheers to Lucy. Cheers to Lionel, pompous prick of the Grammy and the grape. Cheers to Nicole and her pedantic main squeeze. I'm sure that professor crap plays well in D.C., but here in New York we traffic in reality. Jesus Christ, thought Chuck. Maybe he'd better go easy on that third glass of red. It was coalescing nicely with the half a bottle of Lagavulin he'd consumed. By the time they hit the after-dinner drinks he might be dancing naked on the tabletop.

He tucked into the thick bloody slab of tenderloin that Lucy had laid on his plate, alongside the potatoes which he'd surreptitiously loaded up on. He needed to neutralize some of the alcohol pulsing through his blood system or it was going to get ugly. What was Dan prattling on about anyway, competitive bastard, laying claim to some trumped-up sense of artistic empathy with Lionel. Their host may have been a British poseur with one memorable tune and a slightly used conductor's baton, but that was two swings closer than Dan ever had at the plate. If Chuck had to hear one more quip about his goddamned one-act, he might just puke all over Lucy's antique linen tablecloth.

"So, the premise is the subway car from hell that comes to a halt on the Manhattan Bridge, thanks to city budget cuts?" Gray asked politely.

"Well, it's not so much a premise as a setup," replied Dan.

"For what?"

"The characters, all of whom I play. Think *Taking of Pelham* – the original of course — meets *Taxi*."

"And what does one do with this concept, if you don't mind me asking."

Panhandles on the Number 2 express while people bury their heads in their iPads to not have to listen to this crap, thought Chuck.

"I'm going to workshop it first. Really put it through the ringer. I studied at Neighborhood Playhouse, you know. Meisner was simply a genius."

Gray nodded, pretending he had a clue who Meisner was. Nora looked away. She was used to Dan's self-serving meanderings, but she found this thread especially embarrassing in front of The Educated Stranger. Maybe with any luck, Gray wouldn't remember that she was his wife.

"I'm actually developing a Kevin Bacon character."

Oh god, here it comes, thought Nora with thinly veiled disgust.

"I did a film a few years back—."

"A student film," Nora interrupted, casting a silence over the table. *Whups!* She just couldn't help herself.

"An indie film," Dan said, seething inside. "It showed on IFC." Count on Nora to quench his moment.

"We watch IFC all the time," Gray said, trying to reboot Dan's story.

"More wine?" Lionel asked, working his way around the table.

"Anyway, despite the fact my wife has patience for little more than diddling herself to *Tudors* reruns—." He glared at her. "—I got some pretty heady reviews that positioned me as the next Kevin Bacon. Which would not be such a bad thing."

"I found him especially effective in *Mystic River*," Gray

offered, generously.

"My agent," Dan continued, ignoring the sight of Nora's eyeballs rolling into the back of her head like Regan in *The Exorcist*, "thinks if I polish this thing up, we can raise development funds and do a professional reading. Or at the very least, it can get me some casting calls."

"You must have balls of steel to still be at it," Gray said.

"And a wife with a good job," Nora snorted under her breath.

"How about we go refill that meat platter, hon?" Lucy said, steering Nora safely away. The women disappeared into the kitchen, leaving a nice, plump, pregnant pause in the dialogue behind them.

"Well," Lionel said finally. "Jolly good, Dan."

"Yes, it sounds fabulous," Gray added.

"Whatever," Dan muttered. Nothing like having your life's work reduced to a pipe dream by your own wife, he thought to himself. Almost as rich an ego boost as having his mother ask when he was going to get a real job.

Lucy returned with a tray in each hand. "Who wants what?" she asked.

Dan speared another slice of cow.

"You haven't said a word all night," Paula whispered in Chuck's ear. "What are you staring at? Are you drunk?"

"Is this multiple choice?" he replied.

"Don't embarrass me here."

"As opposed to where."

"This is not the time or place," Paula hissed. "I thought you weren't going to drink yourself under the table."

"No, I think your friend Dan reserved that honor for himself."

"Forget it. You can really be an asshole sometimes."

Chuck helped himself to more potatoes as Lucy glided

by, smiling madly at her as he returned the serving spoon to the bowl.

"We're going to lose the house you know."

"What?" Paula asked, when Lucy moved on.

"Oh, nothing. Don't want to make a scene in front of guests now, do we?"

"What are you talking about?" she rasped in a whisper.

"Can't make the payments."

"What payments?"

"The mortgage payments. You know. That check we write at the first of every month? Then there's the Cobra payment. The credit card bills. The Syracuse tuition. By the way, have you told Missy she's going to community college?"

"Jesus Christ Chuck, get a grip."

"Red or white my dear," Lionel asked, towering over Paula and staggering slightly.

Chuck started to slide his glass forward, but Paula firmly laid a hand on his.

"You know, I think we're doing fine."

* * *

The carnage of plates lay stripped and bare like a school of piranha had moved through. A lone brussel sprout remained, Lucy noted. The salad bowl was empty but for an oil slick from the dressing. The meat platter was picked so clean she could put it away as is, were it not for the trickle of runny blood pooling in the bottom.

"Can I get anyone anything else?" Lucy asked.

"One wah-fer thin mint," groaned Dan, invoking Mr. Creosote of Monty Python fame. Nora smiled dutifully. After a brief cooling off session in the kitchen, she had decided to behave. She knew things had gotten out of hand between her and Dan, but this was hardly the place to air her dirty laundry.

"A repast of exquisite proportions, Chef Kaminsky," said Gray.

"I'm glad you enjoyed," Lucy replied.

"Nicole was right. You met and exceeded expectation."

"As have you. Our Nic has really drawn an ace from her second deck."

"Here, here," Gray said, raising his glass. "I am the one who drew the winning hand. Thank you, all – for inviting me into your circle. Though I have to admit, you do have a unique way of greeting someone."

"Do you think I'll be hearing about this for the next twenty years," Nicole commented to no one in particular. She was looking a bit glassy-eyed herself.

"I certainly hope so," said Gray. "Twenty years and beyond." A collective "Ohhhh, isn't that sweet" rose from the table. Nicole nuzzled up close to her beau.

Nora thought she might weep. Or barf. She wasn't sure which.

"Great meal, love," Lionel said.

"And you hit all the right notes on the nutrition scale," Gray added.

"Are you boasting, honey?" Nicole teased.

"Marketing, my dear. There is a difference."

"And what precisely would you be marketing – or boasting – about?" Lucy inquired.

"Gray was recently appointed to the board of Let's Move," Nicole said. She was met with blank stares. "You know. Michelle's thing on childhood obesity?"

"You're referring to *that* Michelle?" Lucy asked.

Nicole nodded. "Her arms are even better in person," she confided.

"You've met Michelle Obama?" Dan asked, barely able

to hide his incredulity.

"And the guy who lives with her," Gray laughed.

"Brilliant," said Lionel. "You do keep it close to the vest then, don't you, man." A sheepish expression crossed Gray's face. Nicole squeezed his arm.

"You don't have to be bashful, sweetheart," she said. "It's a big deal. And these are my best friends in the world."

"Well, I don't want to come off as a snot," he apologized. "You probably all had me pegged for an overbearing academic ass as it is."

"Bollocks that," said Lionel.

"He gets so veddy British when he drinks," explained Lucy.

"No shit, that's fantastic, man," Dan said to Gray, just a tad too enthusiastically, paling in the dim light of the pathetic conversation he'd just been having about his own meager career. Nora looked like she'd been stuffed with the smile pasted on her face.

"How compelling," Lionel said, slowly rimming his wine glass with his index finger. "We nearly turn away a friend of the Obamas from the front door, just because of the color of his skin. What an impressive lot we are."

"Oh Lionel, haven't we beaten that sorry horse to death," said Lucy.

"Barely able to see beyond the pasty white complexion of our privileged noses," he continued, not hearing a word she said. "Professor Barnes, may I propose a toast?"

"It's really just a boilerplate Washington appointment," Gray said, trying to downplay what he had started.

"Friends?" Lionel solicited the full attention of his audience, behaving ever the conductor. Lucy half expected him to pull a baton out of his ass.

"We call ourselves refined bastions of civilization. Pillars of the educated class, empowered to improve the minds of the masses." Chuck nearly spit his wine across the table. Paula nudged him hard enough to dislodge a kidney. Lionel ignored them all. "And yet confronted with a guest of a different shade, we behave no better than the quidnuncs and the louts." He cast his eyes about the room with as much gravitas as if he'd just received a commission from the Berlin Symphony.

"Let our actions not pass unnoticed this evening, Professor. We greeted you from behind a facade of barely muted prejudice. And while you have earned our respect and affection, our warmth and laughter – you were under no obligation to accept us. We did not accept you. In fact, my lovely wife and I damn near shut the door in your face! So please allow me to extend our flimsy apologies. You sir, are a far, far better soul than I."

"My god he can get a bit windy, can't he?" Paula whispered to Nora.

"Been locked in that study too damned long if you ask me."

"Our humble congratulations, and servitude to your noble mission." Lionel tilted a bit as he leaned over to clink glasses with Gray.

"Lovely speech dear," Lucy said, righting her husband as best she could.

"Thank you, Maestro," Gray said. "If I ever need a press secretary, the job's yours."

A brief silence settled over the table, a social hiccup in deference to newfound star power.

"So," Dan said at last. "You've hung out with Obama?"

"Briefly," Gray replied.

"What's he like?" Lucy asked. All eyes turned to Gray. He surveyed his rapt audience with grave contemplation.

"One of the bruthahs fo' sho." Seven extremely Caucasian faces stared back at him. "C'mon people," he laughed. "When are you white folk going to relax?"

Everyone jumped up at once to tackle the cleanup. As the parade of helping hands made a conga line to the kitchen, Chuck excused himself. He found his way to the bathroom and unleashed a stream with a merciful sigh.

God, even their hand towels are luxurious, he thought, pissing endlessly. He stared at the gold leaf wallpaper. So Nicole really came out from her divorce swinging. Walks away with the house and a nice fat alimony check, and whips the whole college gang into a frenzy because she's banging a black guy. Of course he turns out to be Mr. Washington Bigshot. Figures. The rich get richer.

His bladder finally empty, Chuck found his way back to Lionel's study. A quick snort of Lagavulin was what he needed. He grabbed a fresh glass from the bar and poured. Shoot, didn't need that much. Still, he swirled it around the delicate snifter to release the aroma. It barely burned going down. Like drinking out of the bottom of an ashtray. An acquired taste that he was becoming way too familiar with.

He leaned flush against the picture window and stared down fourteen floors to the traffic below on 79th Street. He had not heard one piece of good news in over a year. Job, gone. Career track, toast. Savings, history. He had lost good friends and colleagues on 9/11. Their end had been mercifully quick. The bottomless pit his career had become was no such thing. Paula tried to understand, but how could she? Try explaining to your wife what it feels like to be interviewed for a lowly sales position by a 26-year-old IT vice president. Chuck felt like an extinct species walking into a Chelsea startup office, portfolio tucked under his arm, begging – and what more was it than that? – to an unshaven kid in a Coldplay t-shirt. He made his best pitch. The kid barely looked up from his iPhone.

Chuck took a swig from his snifter. He had put in fourteen years of mind-numbing work to get his family somewhere. To buy the pretty house in Summit; to ride the Direct Express into the heart of the city and be a part of the machine. He had not followed a single one of his dreams. He was not going to hit the game-winning home run or sink the 18th hole putt. He'd never play drums for the E Street Band. No White House appointment for ol' Chuck Dempster. He stared out at the twinkling grid of the Upper East Side. Wealth glistened like Christmas lights from every apartment window. He could reach out and touch it, were it not so far away. He sunk into his own distorted image in the glass. A phone rang. Followed by an uproarious burst of laughter. He wandered back in to explore.

The soirée had reassembled in the living room, guests splayed out like characters in a Toulouse-Lautrec painting, posed across the various surfaces. Lucy was cozied up between Gray and Nicole, fiddling with Gray's kufi while Nicole checked her messages.

"And whom is my child bride texting with?" Gray asked with mock jealousy.

"Child bride? Did I hear that correctly?" Paula asked.

"He likes to call me that," Nicole said, scrolling with one finger. "It's sweet. Makes me feel like I'm about fourteen."

"Ahhh, so no furtive dash to the Justice of the Peace for you two?" Nora asked, perusing books on the windowsill from Lucy and Lionel's personal collection.

"Why mess with a good thing?" Gray said, peering over Nicole's shoulder.

"Hey, no peeking," she objected.

"Secrets to hide, dear?"

"Huge ones," Nicole said. "My ex wants to know if I can do Emily's orthodontist appointment next week. A cameraman who's been accosting me for a freelance gig wants to have coffee. Oh, and look here. My high school reunion committee sent a Save the Date. Shall we alert the media?"

Lionel leaned over the coffee table and topped off Gray's after-dinner drink. "Bloody cell phones," he grumbled to himself. "God help us all if Al Qaeda takes out the grid."

"Oh honey, you're just jealous," Lucy said. "Would you like me to text you? We can all play." She extracted herself from the congestion on the long leather sofa, climbing over Dan in the process. "Oh my lord."

"What?" Lionel said.

"That is too funny."

"What is?" Nora asked, rejoining the group. Dan was hunched over his phone, tapping away like a squirrel with a nut.

"Dan tweets!" Lucy said, unable to avert her gaze from his screen as he tried to hide the evidence.

"You do?" Nora exclaimed with surprise.

"You didn't know?" Lucy said.

"It's for my work," Dan muttered, embarrassed.

"What work?" Nora said, grabbing the phone out of his hand. "You haven't had a job in two years."

"Hey, that's mine."

"Fat chance, bud. If you're tweeting, I'd say you hardly have a leg to stand on." She started to read from Dan's iPhone, aloud. "*Heading 2 din-din with the wife.* Oh, is that what I am. THE wife?"

"Oooh baby," Nicole hooted. Even Chuck smiled from his perch in the window.

"*Near Bacon sighting, 2:25 in Park. Added to script.*" Nora kept scrolling down, scrutinizing the small screen with one eye cocked doubtfully.

"Rehearsing w/Tory next week." She gave Dan a withering look. "Who's Tory?"

"Who cares?" Dan grabbed for his phone. Nora held it above her head and escaped to the other side of the couch. She kept reading. Then her jaw dropped.

"You spent forty-five dollars on that bottle of wine?"

Dan jumped up and grabbed his phone back from Nora angrily. "That's none of your damned business."

"No? How many followers do you have, Dan? How many Tweetie Birds glom on to your narcissistic need to moon the world with the pathetic drivelings from your electronic ass?"

Lucy stepped between them before anyone got beaten senseless with the business end of an iPhone. "I don't think I'd choose to share my private affairs like that," she said diplomatically, trying to gloss things over. Keeping Dan and Nora at bay was becoming a full-time occupation.

"That's not exactly true dear," Lionel said. "You *are* on Facebook."

"Only because a friend shamed me into joining. I didn't even post a recent picture."

"And you still got about a hundred responses. I'm sure all your old grade school conquests are scouring your profile while they frantically masturbate."

"That's revolting," Lucy said.

"My social networking preference," Lionel said, "is sitting in the window with a telescope like Jimmy Stewart in *Rear Window.*"

"Yes honey. Everyone needs to know the depths of your perversion."

"The fourth apartment on the 11th floor looks really good for that," offered Chuck, who had not moved an inch from his post on the radiator hood.

Dan sauntered over to check it out.

"Wait, I'll get the binoculars." Lionel jumped up and plucked them conveniently from under the stereo shelf.

"You have got to be kidding," Nora said.

"He's not," said Lucy.

"Men," said Nicole.

Lionel joined the fraternity at the window with a Bushnell PowerViewer large enough to lead a night raid in the Helmand Province. Chuck grabbed it out of his hand and trained it on the building across the street.

"I can't believe it," Paula said. "You're all sick."

"One might argue that Chuck is the only healthy one in the room," Gray suggested. "At least he's interacting with humanity."

"That's a generous description of a Peeping Tom," Paula said.

"Come on," Lucy interrupted. "Who wants to keep me company in the kitchen?"

* * *

Paula lined up coffee cups on a tray. Nora searched through the cabinets as Lucy rummaged through the fridge.

"Do you have a creamer and sugar bowl?" Nora asked.

"Next cabinet over," Lucy said as she got out a pint of heavy cream. She poured the entire container into a stainless steel mixing bowl and set it under her red enamel KitchenAid mixer. She opened a small plastic Ziploc bag and dumped a few pods out on a board.

"What are those?" asked Paula.

"Fresh vanilla beans. Killer flavor." Lucy used her six-inch paring knife to crack the husks open and scraped the flesh into the bowl. She set the blender on low. The women stood in silence, awed by the sight of pasteurized dairy product transforming itself into frothy peaked waves. When the whipped cream was set, Lucy turned the mixer off. Nora dipped a dainty finger in and sampled.

"You have not lost your touch," she said. "Incredible."

Paula sighed. She hadn't done a dinner party that did not feature cardboard pizza boxes in longer than she could recall. She surveyed the latticework crust of the perfectly browned pie resting on a Blue Willow serving plate. Why was it that Lucy was able to create pies and breads and crab cakes and roasts that looked like they'd just walked off the cover of *Food and Wine*, when she could barely get macaroni and cheese on the table? Was Lucy just born with the perfect gene, or was Paula somehow flawed? She lowered her nose to the runny rhubarb and berries oozing from the piecrust.

"Did you make this, too?" she asked.

"Nope," said Lucy. "Credit where credit is due. That's Lionel's invention."

Paula could barely contain her sense of – was it jealousy? – or merely a combination of too much wine and the fact that her husband had just announced that their life was on the verge of foreclosure. Maybe it *was* time for her to get out of the house. Granted, her resume was a bit thin and dated, but who said salvation was hiding in an office cubicle? Maybe this was a clarion call for real change. What did she love to do? She squinched up her nose in deep thought, but every last idea that came to mind reeked of high school basketball courts, cheerleader tryouts, carpooling, and bagged lunches. Had she really relegated her entire persona to the raising of two New Jersey school kids? Was secretary of the Summit PTA the top of the heap?

"Don't be too impressed," Lucy said, interrupting

Paula's train of thought. "I had to move heaven and earth to get Lionel to make it."

"You guys are too much."

Lucy flashed a wan smile back at her, secretly wondering if too much was really enough.

* * *

"Do you think Lucy and Nicole ever experimented?" Dan asked. The men had retired to the study, where they were holding court on the comfortably worn leather couch. It looked like a World War Two bomber jacket with legs. Several bottles of the good stuff had been cracked, new crystal rolled out for the occasion.

"Experimented with what?" Lionel asked.

"You know. Chicks. Each other. The whole hasbian thing?"

"Excuse me?"

"I believe he is asking if your wife and my girlfriend have engaged in shared erotic behavior," Gray said.

Lionel put an arm around Dan's shoulder. "Lucy's right. Your mind *is* in the gutter."

"Oh lighten up Lionel. Tell me you wouldn't dig it if Lucy hadn't been to the rodeo once with some hot little bi number in her illustrious past."

"I prefer not to think about my wife's illustrious past," he said, a bolt of forgotten insecurity cutting through the alcohol and rocketing him straight back to the uncomfortable place it had taken him all evening to forget.

"Nora totally did the chick thing in college," Dan mused. "Very hot."

"Lovely," Lionel said. "Perhaps you should post it on Twitter."

"So," Gray interjected, changing the subject. "Enlighten me, Chuck. What's it really like out there on the street?"

"Grim," replied Chuck, perched on the thickly rolled leather arm of the couch, twirling a fresh drink. "Don't believe a thing you read. The numbers are lying."

"How so?" Gray asked.

"We're all being manipulated by the Fed and the media. There's no comeback going on. Guys like me have dropped off the statistical map."

"But you're bloody good," Lionel said. "You could sell charcoal in hell. Surely there's a job out there for you."

"You'd think. I see ex-bankers from the 7:42 slicing deli at the local Wegman's. People are clamoring for something to do. Anything! Trust me, I know."

Gray tilted his snifter, studying the thick runny legs his fifteen-year-old cognac left on the delicate blown glass. "No doubt a Pyrrhic victory for the Occupy crowd." he remarked. He set his drink down. "Nicole tells me you architected the software that put Wall Street into the ionosphere?"

"That's a stretch," Chuck said. "I sold enterprise systems to the big finance houses, back in the ice age. Now I'm thinking about building a hothouse in our backyard to grow year-round tomatoes."

"Locavore is in," Gray said.

"Tell that to my mortgage banker."

Gray adjusted his kufi. "You know, ultimately there is going to be a revolt. It's just a matter of time."

"Riiiight," Chuck said. "12,000 men in Brooks Brothers khakis waving their BlackBerries in solidarity."

"I was thinking a little less orderly than that. More along the lines of Watts after Rodney King."

"Gray, not to bring up old baggage," Chuck said, "and with all due respect to your academic prowess – but we're not black. White people don't riot. We eat Haagen Dazs. We coach soccer. We detail our Windstars. I don't quite see The Million White Guy March."

"That would be rather ugly," Lionel said. No one disagreed.

* * *

The sound of traffic rose up from the street. Lucy sat exposed to the elements, twelve floors above on the apartment's tiny parapet terrace. She had climbed out the window – the only access to the space – to get some air. The weather had changed and an unseasonably warm southeasterly breeze tugged at her hair. Across the way, a still life of triple-paned safety glass windows shielded all those strangers in the building they'd stared out on for years. The most important men in her life had just paid deference to the view, glued to the anonymous action through a powerful pair of binoculars. What could that reveal besides a random sighting of human intercourse, she wondered. What was it with men and their porn, anyway? They didn't make a long enough lens to really allow you to peer into people's lives. That would be way too disturbing.

A clap of thunder startled her. She craned her neck a bit and looked out over the Park. Lightning flashed in the distance. Whenever she snuck out the bedroom window to the terrace, she looked west. She imagined New Jersey, and Pennsylvania, Ohio, Chicago, and the unspeakably vast beyond, all of it spread out in endless fields of fruited plain. Out there you could have three acres, a McMansion, a porch swing, your own personal sauna and a sixty-inch flat screen TV in your thousand square foot bedroom, and the mall. New York was its own peculiar island: crowded, snarky, self-contained, self-absorbed, and yet nothing could drag her away. She had only considered escape once, long ago, when Lionel's inadvertent fortune came in and she entreated him with every last ounce of love and fervor to multiply with her; to grow their family and expand their empire of three. *We could build you a studio. Isaac could have a basketball court in the driveway. I could have my herb garden and you could have that Jaguar XKE you always dreamed of.* Her words had fallen on deaf ears. Had she ever really forgiven him?

A loud peal of laughter erupted from inside. The party was a success. From high above in their Manhattan minaret, she and Lionel had pulled it off. The beef had turned out fabulously. Lionel's pie was devoured. Dessert had dissolved into a quartet of disparate groups, snippets of conversation sprinkled around the maze of the apartment. She could hear the smatterings floating out the window above the constant hum of the city below.

She reached inside her bra and pulled out the joint that she had snatched from her dresser drawer. She unearthed the plastic disposable Bic lighter that she kept hidden beneath a loose brick. She took a deep drag, letting the smoke penetrate her. She closed her eyes and waited for the rush. It was good pot. Thank God for actor friends. Dan kept her stocked for the pinch. She much preferred a leisurely joint to the collection of expensive single malts that Lionel favored.

She blew the smoke out in a thin steady line, watching it stream into the night sky like a small horizontal exclamation point. The authoritarian tones of Gray filtered above the din. No shock, Nicole had landed on her feet. The evening had been such a blur that she and Nic had barely gotten a moment to speak. She'd have to intercept her tomorrow before she hightailed it back to D.C. Maybe Lionel could amuse Gray while the girls stole an espresso. It certainly seemed like the two men had hit it off.

Lucy closed her eyes and let the weed infiltrate her brain. What had driven Nicole to the brink with Bill? He was handsome, sweet, funny. A great Dad and an able provider. What crossed wire in their personal chemistry had pushed Nicole so far that she ultimately leapt without a parachute? How despondent she must have been, Lucy thought. Or brave. Would *she* have the nerve to carry that off? She wasn't so sure. Was it worse to carry the secrets that chipped away at the core, or extract yourself from the quicksand of marriage?

"Mind if I join you?"

"Shit," Lucy said nearly jumping out of her skin. "You scared me."

"Jeez, Luce. A little wound up, are we?" Nicole put one foot up on the windowsill and hoisted herself through the open bedroom window. She took a deep sniff of the air. "Mmmm. I figured I might find you out here."

Lucy took Nicole's hand as she nimbly climbed onto the terrace. There was just enough room for the two of them. Nicole leaned her back against the thick stone wall that shored up the face of the building. An errant stumble and it was twelve floors down, express.

"You want a hit?" Lucy asked.

"Is the Pope Catholic?" Nicole took a drag from the joint, holding it between her two fingers like it was a Virginia Slim. "Ahhh, now that's more like it." She handed it back to Lucy. The breeze picked up. Thunder rumbled throatily in the distance. The girls sat in silence for a moment, enjoying the view.

"He's really nice," Lucy said at last.

"He's different than anyone I've ever been with."

Lucy nodded. Coming from Nicole, that was high praise. She had been with more men than Lucy could begin to count.

Lucy always attributed it to her exotic good looks. Not to mention the fact that she was unencumbered by such limitations as, say, discretion. When Lucy and Nicole had roomed together, their fifth floor walkup on Second Avenue had two bedrooms the size of walk-in closets and a constant soundtrack of M15 buses rumbling down the avenue. Lucy had spent more nights alone than she cared to remember, watching Saturday Night Live or falling asleep to a Lori Colwin column in *Gourmet*, while Nicole was out with one of her architects or bankers or some tortured poet. Nicole did not play favorites. Once, when she had returned at daybreak from yet another successful tryst, Lucy had asked, "How do you do it?"

"Do what?" Nicole had replied, puzzled.

"Sleep with guys so easily."

"Honey, it's just a dick." *Well there you go*, thought Lucy. The answer to all life's mysteries.

Nicole took another pull off the joint. The women sat quietly for a while, stoned, like gargoyles atop their cornice bivouac, watching out over the city. "Do you think you'll ever get married again?" Lucy asked.

"And ruin everything?" Nicole's reply spit out as fast as a crisp twenty from an ATM machine. "We've got enough going on as it is. Two homes. Five children. His job. My job. And now this new commission? Our plates are plenty full. I'm not sure how marriage would make it any better."

"You've got a point," Lucy agreed. "Though you guys do look amazing together. God help us if you ever accidentally had a kid. That would be one precious bronze baby."

"I'd never thought about that."

How Nicole, Lucy mused. It would be just like her to wake up pregnant one morning and decide what the hell.

Surprise, Gray. Guess what we're having? Her best friend was the one they'd invented the deep end for.

"Are you okay, Lucy?"

"Huhhh? Yeah. I'm good."

"Uh huh." Nicole looked unconvinced. "Are you and Lionel having problems?"

"No silly. We couldn't be better."

"Those famous last words," observed Nicole dryly, "before calling everyone you know for the name of a good divorce lawyer."

Lucy's thoughts zoned in and out through the cannabis fog, the breeze wafting humid currents across the terrace. It was tempting to open up, but she was afraid. Afraid to share the truth: the emptiness that tormented her since Isaac had gone off. The depression that permeated her husband. The new routine they had both settled into, knocking about the empty apartment, not strangers, but not exactly partners either. She and Lionel weren't bad and they weren't good. They just were. Wasn't that what marriage was supposed to be after twenty years, anyway? Why rock the boat? Maybe she should just tear up the Harlem address and erase it from her mind. She tried to remember if she had set the coffee to brew. She had a really nice buzz going.

"Lucy?"

"Nothing to tell, sweetie," she lied. "Lionel's great. Isaac's great. I've got the foundation work. I'm chairing the fall event at St. Jude's. I still do pro bono work for the Children's Defense Fund. I've been volunteering at Ronald McDonald House. Then there's all those City Harvest events. Did I tell you I'm on their Board?" Lucy gushed like a broken hydrant. Nicole stared at her like she'd come unglued.

Lucy relit the remains of the extinguished joint and took a quick hit. Laughter spilled out from behind them through the bedroom window. She handed the roach to Nicole and rose from the rough stone surface. She placed her palm on her friend's cheek for a lingering moment and then before Nic could say another word, she eased herself back inside.

* * *

The party had shifted into full throttle. All semblance of choreography and menu had dissolved into a pastiche of open bottles, refilled glasses and shouted conversation. Lucy floated into the kitchen in search of the after-dinner cheeses. She found the board atop the counter where she had left it to warm to room temperature. The St. Andre – a true heartstopper in all its triple crème glory – was just right. Its innards ran down its side like molten lava. Perfect. She reached into the fridge and pulled out a chilled plate full of meticulously selected fruits: kiwis, strawberries, raspberries, and a collection of fresh California figs. Somewhere, she had stowed a box of fancy crackers, but the pot had her all disoriented and she could not be bothered to find them. There, on the counter. She fetched the remains of an Amy's baguette and threw the crusts haphazardly into a bowl and waltzed merrily back to the living room.

She joined Lionel on his favorite chair, where he was regaling Gray with a story about his long lost London youth. She kissed her husband openly on the mouth.

"My my," Lionel said. "And where has my delicate flower been hiding?"

"Nic and I slipped out for a breath of fresh air."

"I believe a *cloud* of fresh air would be the operative term here," he said knowingly. "A good hostess would have offered to share."

"I think the guests are quite happy," Lucy said in a

singsongy voice. "No need to upset the delicate balance."

Nicole wandered back in barefoot, her Jimmy Choos hanging off one finger. She flopped into the crook of Gray's arm like a teenage girlfriend, head on his shoulder, a hand on his thigh. Her pretty bare feet danced circles in the air. Paula sat stiffly in a wingback chair, glaring at her. She could smell the stench of weed from halfway across the room. *Spoiled brat, she thought. It wasn't bad enough that Nicole dumped her kids in favor of a little helping of extramarital sex. Now she had to relive her youth, getting high like a college sophomore? The strong scent of urban privilege drifted through Lucy's living room. Nice of the girls to ask her to join.*

Dan was performing a skit from his one-act for Chuck. He seemed to be playing an enraged taxi driver confronting a befuddled matronly patron. John Leguizamo meets Bette Midler. Chuck feigned mild amusement, a glazed expression on his face, no doubt fortified by the fact that his glass had not dipped below empty since he'd arrived.

Paula reached with distaste around Nicole's twirling toes to the fruit plate on the ottoman and snagged a fig. Lucy smiled contentedly. Her work was done. A bleating sound emanated from the coffee table. Lionel shot up, nearly ejecting Lucy in the process.

"Bloody phone. We're not answering it."

"Whatever," Lucy said. "It's kind of late. Just see who it is."

Lionel plucked the offending unit from the clutter. He glanced at the illuminated screen.

"See? All crap. Some meaningless drivel from Match.com." He held up the device. The room fell silent.

"Hello?" he said, waving the phone about like a raffle ticket, looking for its rightful owner. Lucy tried to flash him a message with her eyes, but it missed the mark. Lionel's life, she was only too familiar, was conducted on a highly intellectual plane: cloistered and internal, uncluttered by contact with anyone resembling a dating, single human being. It was possible, she realized, that he was completely unaware. That made him the only one.

"Just put it down, Lionel," Lucy begged. "Who wants to try this orgasmic triple crème?" She might as well have smeared it across her naked breasts. The die was cast.

"Nora?" Dan asked. "Isn't that your phone?"

Nora chuckled uncomfortably. "Don't be silly."

"I'm not," said Dan.

"Why would I be getting a message from some dating service?"

"Ya got me!"

Even Lionel, through the Lagavulin haze, realized his mistake. He slipped the iPhone back onto the coffee table and tried to make it disappear beneath a plate of smoked Gouda and a clutter of wrinkled napkins. He picked up an ornate knife and sliced a thick hunk of Brillat-Savarin. "*Fromage*, anyone?"

"No, this sounds fun," Dan said. "Time for a party game." He retrieved Nora's phone and held it out to her. "Shall we see who it is, honey?" Discomfort spread through the room like gas. The only sound was the tinkling of ice as Chuck tried to suck the last remains of whisky from his glass.

Nora stared Dan down, oblivious to the rest of the faces focused on her. "You know the password," she said. Her face contorted into a challenging sneer. "Knock yourself out."

Dan stood on the cusp, caught in a trap of his own making. There was nowhere to run and hide. He tapped in her digits. He studied the text.

"Greg has sent you a message," he announced brightly. "How nice. Shall we read it?"

"C'mon Dan," Lucy said, reaching for the phone.

"Enough."

"No." He held the phone away from Lucy. "We're all friends here."

"Go ahead," Nora said, issuing a dare. She stared at her husband. The gloves were off.

All eyes were on Dan as he clicked through the message. He read aloud.

"I hope you're as sexy in person as you are in prose. Let's meet. Coffee next week? Call me."

Dan stared at his wife. Lionel sighed audibly, his cheeks puffing out like a tuba player. Paula gazed at Nora, her jaw agape. Even Chuck put his drink down.

"So?" Dan asked Nora. "Are you?"

"Am I what?" she replied coldly.

"As sexy in person as you are in prose? Because frankly, I can't remember the last time I got a letter from you."

"Fuck you Dan."

"Yes, that seems to be the operative word here."

"You wish. Because then you'd have a nice tidy little scene to script for your stupid goddamned play."

"Oh, is that what this is all about? I'm pursuing my passion, so you need to pursue yours? A little foreign cock to light the home fires?"

"Fuck you again! I don't spend my days and nights waltzing through bad acting classes with tart-titted groupies named Tory and Monique."

"No, you're too busy surfing the Internet for dickheads named Greg."

"Guys, please, come on," Lucy begged in vain. Dan's face had turned red as a ripe tomato.

"What did you write in your ad, Nora? Biological clock thumping like a drum seeks willing sperm donor for chitchat and fellatio?"

Nora lifted her wine glass threateningly and then reconsidered. An original Jasper Johns hung on the wall behind the couch. She set the glass down and snatched her phone back from Dan's hand.

"How would you know the first thing about what I need? You're too blinded by any conceit that your pathetic little one-act will turn a single eyeball in this town. Kevin Bacon my ass. He hasn't done anything good since *Footloose*, anyway. You're washed up, Dan. You're too old. It's a kids' game. You missed the boat. Shove that in your biological pipe and smoke it!"

The front door slammed so hard on her way out that the chandelier rocked, its Tiffany glass chimes dangling a merry tune in her wake.

- 21 -
JUST DESSERTS

Skrik-ak. Skrik-ak. Skrik-ak. Skrik-ak. Christ, how long had the record been skipping at its end, Lucy wondered, lifting the needle from the disk. No one seemed to notice the difference.

"Well," Lionel said at last. "That was jolly good fun. Who needs a drink?"

Lucy shot him a look that stopped him dead in his tracks. Her eyes flashed like cutlery. Nicole reached for her friend but Lucy pulled away like she'd been stung. The silence in the room was deafening.

What the hell was going on? Dan paced like a madman back and forth across the living room, oblivious to Lucy's hand on his shoulder, trying to guide him back down to the couch. What the fuck. This wasn't happening. If he had not read the text message himself he wouldn't have believed it in a million years. His wife was on the prowl? Jesus, hadn't they just made love in the shower a mere few hours ago? That was no sham. He had felt her whole body shudder as she came. And yet there was the incontrovertible evidence, spelled out in black and white. The plain truth delivered through the trusty servers of America's largest dating service.

"*Are you as sexy in person as you are in prose?*"

He dissected the words in his feverishly racing brain. Cheesy romantic pablum, that's what it was. The desperate ramblings of some divorced prick, probably a writer, based on the selection of verbiage. A bad writer. Unpublished, of course. Who else could come up with copy so desperate and overheated. Not that he gave a shit about the bastard's literary calisthenics?

"*I would love to meet.*"

No getting around that. Whoever this Greg bastard was, he was responding in kind to words that his wife had put out there. "I would love to meet." Meet YOU. You, Nora, who for some insane reason reached out to HIM!

"*Coffee next week?*"

Sure. A discreet rendezvous, a little heavy eye contact, followed by the Searing Personal Confessionals portion of the program. Hand-holding over espressos at Café Lalo in the middle of the afternoon. How far could that be from Nora traipsing upstairs to his apartment – Fuck, what if he was loaded? Fat with filthy Wall Street cash. What if they were gliding skyward thirty floors up to his highrise bachelor pad, where he would unbutton her blouse, peel off her jeans, unwrap her like an expensive truffle and, oh dear God, he couldn't bear the thought of it. All that was left was the lawyers and the moving van.

"Dan?" Lucy intruded on his internal soliloquy. She took him by the shoulders and plunked him down hard on the couch.

He sank into the cushion and slipped into a breathing exercise, trying not to hyperventilate. Lionel smeared a thick gooey dab of St. Andre onto a chunk of baguette and took a large bite. Gray sat in an easy chair, watching from a supervisory position. Nicole perched on the arm of the chair, her face scrunched up in deep conjecture. Chuck fetched a fresh scotch for Dan. The men needed to stick together.

"Can someone please tell me what just happened?" Dan asked, twirling the ice in his drink. He looked as forlorn as a wet Schnauzer.

"I'm not really sure," said Lucy.

"You didn't know?"

"Know what?"

"That my wife is having an affair."

"Whoa, hold the phone. Who said anything about an affair?"

"Hello! Did anyone else hear the words in that note? It didn't sound like afternoon tea to me."

Dan was greeted with silence. "See?"

"There's got to be some kind of misunderstanding," Lucy said.

"I agree," chimed in Gray. "Why would she let you read such an incriminating message?"

"Because she had no choice," Dan said.

"Good point," offered Chuck.

"You're a help," Paula said, glaring at him.

Chuck shrugged. The whole night had been a whisky blur. This felt like one more tumbler under the bridge. Paula's friends were all a little nuts as far as he was concerned. Wasn't he the one who had just wanted to stay home and watch the Yankees game?

"I think we're all overreacting," Lucy said. "Come on Dan. Do you have a reason in the world to suspect that Nora is seeing someone?"

"No more than I think you are."

"Lucy?" Lionel asked, one eyebrow shooting up like a comma.

"Good God!" Things were getting out of hand.

"Maybe he's an old friend," Gray suggested.

"Who she happened to bump into on Match?" Nicole replied. "No way. It doesn't add up. I think the question is, what the hell was she doing on Match in the first place?" Her gaze drilled straight into Dan.

"Why are you all looking at me?" he asked.

"Well it's not like your wife stuck around for the Q & A," Nicole said, separating a plump Concord grape from its stem. She popped it into her mouth.

Lucy put an arm around her crestfallen buddy. "I have a gut feeling this isn't what it seems. Maybe you should go home and talk to her."

Dan looked around the room at his compadres. Chuck and Paula. Lionel and Lucy. Nic and Gray. Judging by the depth of the pained expressions on their faces, you'd think he'd just been diagnosed with something horrible. The last thing he needed was a roomful of gratuitous advice. *Fuck it.* He wasn't going to sit around like a victim, wallowing in self-pity. Since when did a little rejection get him down, anyway? Hell, he was a fighter. No one could ever accuse him of buckling up and folding. Screw Nora. Screw his agent. Screw them all. It was Saturday night in the greatest city in the world and it wasn't even midnight. The eager chum of singles Manhattan was just starting to thrash. Time to do a little bottom feeding. Two could play at this game.

"I'm out of here," he announced, bounding from the couch.

"Where are you going," Lucy asked.

"Out."

"Are you going to be okay?"

"Hell yeah." Dan ignored the sea of faces staring up at him like he'd grown a third eye. He did not look back as he exited the living room. Lucy followed him.

"Great party, Luce," he said, fumbling with the chain on the front door. She put one hand on his shoulder, worried.

"You sure I can't make you a coffee or something?"

He shook his head. "I just need some space."

"You'll let me know what happens?"

He kissed her on the cheek. "I'll text you." He disappeared down the hall.

Lucy bolted the door shut and returned to the inner circle. A pall hung over the room.

"That was not good," said Lucy.

"No," agreed Nicole. "It never is."

Paula shot Nicole a sharp look.

"You want some help straightening up, Luce?" Nicole asked, just a decibel too loudly. She met Paula's stare like a bull in a pasture.

"You bet," Lucy said.

As if someone had released a steam valve, everyone jumped up and started hauling the detritus of the evening into the kitchen. In no time at all every last surface was stacked so full there was nowhere to lay down so much as a stem glass.

"Do you have a dishwasher?" Chuck asked, confused.

"Under the counter," Lucy said. She popped open the camouflaged door to their industrial-sized Miele.

"Holy cow," he said, loading several large serving bowls into the cavernous machine. "You guys could park a Mini Cooper in here."

"It came with the place," Lucy said apologetically. It did reek a bit of overkill, she knew. What's more, ever since Isaac had gone off to school, her culinary machinations had been dropping off precipitously. Something about slaving in the kitchen for an hour to set two lonely plates on their oversized dining room table. She and Lionel had been living on takeout: getting by for days on waxy cardboard cartons housing leftover curry, beef and broccoli, Szechuan string beans, and greasy lo mein. The once busy dish-scouring appliance now took a week to fill with one environmentally responsible load. At least tonight it was going to earn its keep.

"Why don't you women take a break," Lionel offered. "There's no room in here anyway." The kitchen had become as crowded as a rush hour Number 6 Train. The women obliged, traipsing out and leaving the men behind.

They worked in silence, ignoring the elephant in the room – the fate of their fallen comrade. Gray took a handful of plates and placed them in the carefully architected racks of the gaping Miele. "My first wife left me because I had the audacity to inform her that she couldn't load a dishwasher," he announced, breaking the ice.

"No shit," Chuck chimed in. "Paula loads four dinner plates, a fork, maybe the colander – and then she turns the goddamned machine on. Guess who's left with all the pots and pans for the next morning."

"Amazing, isn't it?" Gray concurred.

"It's payback," said Lionel, jumping on the domestic injustice bandwagon. He scrutinized a goo-covered cheese board, and then shrugging, swabbed the last bit off with his finger and licked it clean. "Bloody hell that's good. Have to double my dose of Lipitor tonight." He tossed the board in the overflowing sink.

"My second wife didn't cook," Gray said, "and I've got to tell you, after putting up with my first wife's overblown epicurean aspirations, it was a relief. Spared a lot of drama."

"How many wives have you had?" Lionel asked, loading the silverware into a top rack laid out as orderly as a shrink's desk.

"Two that count. Number three doesn't get a lot of ink."

"Nice. Nicole know about her?" Chuck asked.

"Marginally. She was a bounceback. Had to get that out of my system." Gray scraped the remains of the roast potatoes into the brushed steel, twelve-gallon, foot-operated waste bin. "Obviously you haven't been divorced yet."

"No," Chuck said. "I thought I'd try a devastating run of unemployment first. You know, blaze the trail before I took on the big stuff?"

"Hmmm. Smell that?" Lionel said, aiming his nose with Hoover-like accuracy in the direction of the hallway.

"What?" asked Gray.

Lionel put a fatherly arm around him. "Just don't inhale."

The open windows did little to dispel the blue cloud of pot smoke as it drifted through the room. *Short of a lava lamp and some Grateful Dead bootlegs we could all be back in college*, thought Lucy. The survivors of the evening had gathered in Lionel's study, lounging about the cozy space like slackers in a frat house. Lucy handed the joint off to Nicole, who took a focused, slurping puff. Holding her breath, she held the joint out to Paula between her thumb and forefinger. Paula accepted

Nicole directed a thin blue stream like a contrail towards the ceiling. "What I don't get," she said when she was able to breathe again, "is the whole Match.com angle. I mean it's one thing to stumble into an affair. It's another to actively go seeking it."

"Yes, I'd imagine that's right in your sweet spot," Paula said, blowing out a flume of smoke. Heads spun. She shrugged. *Good pot.*

"Excuse me?" Nicole said, staring in disbelief.

"No, nothing. Forget about it."

"Forget about what – your extraordinary lack of tact, or your holier-than-thou attitude?" Nicole asked.

"I have no idea what you're talking about," Paula replied innocently.

"No? You don't think I haven't picked up on your

snotty little eye rolls and chirps all night?"

"You'll have to take that up with the guilt police," Paula said. She was way beyond giving a shit.

"Screw you, Paula. When were you anointed queen of the self-righteous? Or do they hand out superior attitudes with EZ Pass in your neck of the woods?"

"Go right ahead, Nic. I'm sure it's easy to sit in judgment when your own kids come about twelfth after your sexual needs."

"Oh yeah, excuse me. I forgot. Out there in the 'burbs you all sublimate *your* sexual needs into twenty-pound sacks of cedar mulch."

"We don't call it sublimation, honey. We call it raising a family."

"Guys!" Lucy sighed. She hoped they didn't start throwing plates. Fortunately, the men chose just that moment to waltz into the Ladies Tea and Narcotics Klatch.

Gray sized up the marijuana situation. "If this turns up on Twitter you realize my political career is over." He declined the weed and shuffled over to the window to stay downwind of trouble.

Lionel made no such pretense, taking an enormous hit. Lucy gave him a cockeyed look. For a guy who claimed to have no interest in getting high, he sure seemed comfortable toking away. Maybe he'd been secretly poking around her stash. She wondered what else he'd been snooping about.

"Problem, honey?" Lionel asked, interrupting her stoned reverie.

"What?" She had burrowed so deeply into her private thoughts that she didn't even realize she was glowering at him.

"You're obsessing about Dan, aren't you?"

"And Nora," she added.

"Yes, Dan and Nora. Our own little George and Martha."

"Who are George and Martha?" Paula asked.

"Who's Afraid of Virginia Woolf," Nicole said. And then on Paula's blank stare: "The Edward Albee play?"

Excuse me for breathing you little bitch, thought Paula. "Thanks for the Cliff Notes," she said. "I'm still working my way through *50 Shades of Gray*."

Gray's antennae perked up at Paula's sulfurous tone. "That is a shame about Dan and Nora," he said, attempting to defuse the tension. "A most unfortunate incident."

"Is that what you call cheating on your husband?" Paula said sharply to him. "An unfortunate incident?" Apparently everyone was fair game now.

Nicole slid over to the window, coming to Gray's rescue. "There's quite a line between cheating and what Nora did," she said

"I don't suppose lying crosses the line in your book, either, as long as Nora keeps her clothes on."

"What the hell is your problem?" Nicole said. "You've never lied to Chuck? About anything?"

"Not like that."

"You pose an interesting ethical dilemma," Gray said, scratching his chin. "What white lies do we *all* tell to ballast our relationships?"

"Oh dear God, enough with your pompous bullshit pronouncements already," Paula said.

Gray blanched.

"Have they checked the drinking water out in Jersey for bitch residue lately?" Nicole asked.

"Please you guys?" Lucy said.

"Why lie at all?" Lionel interrupted.

All heads turned. He had been watching from the

sidelines, uncharacteristically silent. He rose from his perch on the sideboard. "Do we all lead such lives of quiet desperation that we have to burrow into a hive of fabrications, just to hold up the walls?" He stared at Lucy with the freighted look of a man on a mission. She stared back at him, crouched on her emotional haunches. If a fight was what he wanted.

"Everyone lies," Nicole cut in. She aimed the burning joint in her hand at Paula like a dagger. "What do you tell Chuck every afternoon when he pours that first martini? 'Proud of you, hon. Who needs a job anyway?'"

Paula did not respond.

"What about you, Chuck? Do you think anyone in this room doesn't know you're a drunk?"

"Jesus Nic," Lucy said.

"Don't *Jesus* me, Lucy. I'm not playing favorites. Ask Gray." She cast her eye toward him. "Did you even want to come tonight, honey? *Do we really have to hang out with a bunch of white, upper-middle-class liberals prattling on about their so-called egalitarianism, nestled in their wealth on the Upper East Side?*" Nicole did a superb imitation of her academic paramour. The air in the apartment had grown as brittle as a Wheat Thin. The joint was burning down to nothingness in Nicole's hand. Gray tried to remove it, but she pulled away.

"I know what you all think of me," Nicole said. "So I won't win Mother of the Year. Too fucking bad. At least my kids will grow up in an honest household. And I can live with that. If Nora's so goddamned unhappy in her marriage that she surfs the Web for a little action, good for her. Get her ya-ya's out. Sometimes the truth hurts. Maybe she's doing Dan a big favor." Nicole gazed about the room. "Which one of you has the balls to do that?"

She surveyed the group for a response. No hands shot

up. She had spoken her piece.

Gray gently extracted the roach from Nicole's thumb and forefinger and stubbed it out in the ashtray. He put one arm around her. He turned to the faces in the room. "That, is why my beloved is *behind* the camera," he said, kissing her forehead.

"Maybe she should have her own show," Lionel said, "because frankly, I couldn't agree more with her every word."

He stared pointedly at his wife. Chuck studied the bottom of his glass as if a tadpole had miraculously appeared in it. Gray nodded politely at Lionel. *My these white people have too much time on their hands*, he thought.

"To Nicole," Lionel said, his words slurring. "For having the temerity to tell the truth." He raised his glass with a gimlet eye toward Lucy.

"Fuck you Lionel." Lucy's words rang out like a rimshot.

"Pardon me?"

"Keep your infantile suspicions to yourself. I'm not screwing my internist. I haven't blown the doorman. And I'm not surfing dating websites. Okay?"

"No," he said after a long pause. "With your looks and intelligence, you wouldn't have to, would you."

Ohhhh forget it. She'd had her fill. Her aching, tortured husband had gone round the bend. It was way too late for appeasement now. There was nowhere good this conversation could go. Lucy rose from the couch.

"Who wants coffee?" she asked in a resigned voice, waving the white flag.

"Yes, that'll solve everything," Lionel said.

"Well, it will have to do for now," Lucy replied. Three aspirin, a huge glass of water and twelve hours sleep was more like it.

The jarring bleat of a cell phone from the next room

startled them all.

"Jesus, Joseph and Mary," Lucy said.

They all hurried back to the living room. The hunt was on.

"That's mine," Chuck said, scooping it up. He cupped the phone in his hand. "Hello? Wait. Hang on a sec. You're breaking up." He took the call by the window.

Lucy started clearing glasses. Gray joined her. Paula ignored them both, staring at her husband at the far side of the room. Chuck nodded several times, one hand over his other ear to hear. He returned, phone in hand, hanging idly by his side. His face was ashen and he swiped at his hair, sweaty on his forehead.

"We've got to go."

"What's wrong?" Paula asked with a look only a mother could summons. Everyone froze.

"There's been an accident. Missy's in the hospital."

"No!"

"Oh God." Lucy set a handful of coffee mugs down on the table with a crash.

"Is she okay?" Paula asked in a whisper.

"I'm not sure." Chuck was already at the coat closet as he spoke. "She's at Summit General."

"What do you mean you're not sure?" The high-pitched panic in Paula's voice was palpable.

"They wouldn't say. They just said she's been transported to the ER and we need to get there as soon as possible."

"Who's *they?*" Paula asked.

"The Union County Sheriff's Office."

The air sucked out of the room. Paula's jaw began to quiver uncontrollably. Lucy reached out toward her. She flinched like a shock had been administered, her hand flitting and patting at something unseen. Chuck was pulling on his blazer.

"What can we do?" Lionel asked. He blocked Chuck's way in the foyer. "How about I call you a car service?"

"No. I'm okay to drive."

"We'll drive you," Lucy said.

"I'm fine. C'mon Paula. Let's go."

They left without goodbyes, the door banging shut behind them. A muffling vacuum lingered in their wake. The hallway chandelier cast a bright light on stricken faces. No one spoke. It seemed, at last, it had all been said.

A few moments later, Lucy stood barefoot in the twelfth floor hallway, the front door propped ajar as she watched the elevator rattle open. First Gray disappeared from sight, then Nicole, her hand raised in a silent farewell. *Call me*, she lip-synched, and then she was gone too. The clanging of the elevator gate rang in Lucy's ears as she walked back into the apartment. She pushed the heavy door closed. The silence was overwhelming. Lionel was nowhere to be seen.

Despite all the cleanup, there was still ample evidence of the affair. A hunk of cheese sagged oily and half-eaten on a plate by the Portuguese bowl. A whisky tumbler sat with its dead brown water next to the glowing blue stereo lamp. A candle burned low in its tarnished silver holder, the wick twisting eerily in the breeze from the open window. The smell of marijuana smoke hung in the air.

Lucy double-bolted the front door and fastened the chain. She padded back into the living room. The remains of the evening could wait. She turned off the lights, casting the apartment into the gaslit yellow darkness that passed for night in Manhattan. She felt the tears well up in her eyes. The party was over. She was all alone.

Part Three
Nightcap

- 22 -
NORA

Damn you, Dan, she thought. *Goddamn you!*

The apartment was empty. Cluttered, tired, dusty: scattered with magazines, dated *Backstages*, *Times Arts & Leisure* sections, stacks of *People*, *Variety* clippings, screenplays that friends had written and begged him to read. He always obliged. *Damn your confidence, Dan. Why couldn't you just quit like all the others? You're nearly forty for Chrissakes. Too old to be screwing around with auditions and staged readings and one-act masturbatory fantasies. Guys your age play golf, consider their savings, plan for their financial future. Ha! What future? You decided to reinvent while everyone else was planning for retirement.*

She felt the beginnings of a migraine coming on. It didn't help that she'd drunk about three bottles of wine over the course of the evening. If nothing else, Lucy had outdone herself, as usual. Some party, Nora thought. Pity she had become the main course.

She heard the front door of the building slam, five floors below. The musty tenement was about as soundproof as a prison block, more suited to college students than any reasonable facsimile of adults. If that was Dan returning home, what was she going to say? Could she have been more busted?

Drunken laughter filtered up through the hall as a large group of Saturday night revelers came clumping up the stairs. Not Dan. She was relieved. Lucy's innocent soirée had unearthed a shit storm of trouble, that was for sure. Jesus.

"I hope you're as sexy in person as you are in prose. Let's meet. Coffee next week? Call me." His note was followed by ten digits. The key to her downfall, a phone call away.

How pathetic, she thought. Suddenly, Greg's words looked as immature as an overwrought teenager's poem. All the surreptitious evenings of game playing, and then the tortured hours awaiting a reply? Now it seemed like a bad joke. She had spent weeks building up to this moment. What did she expect, George Clooney to come waltzing in and sweep her off her feet? She, of all people, should know the difference between the thin pages of scripted drama versus the humiliating reality show her life had just become. Greg was a legally separated plastic surgeon with two kids and a sailboat on a lake somewhere in Connecticut. His wife got the Upper West Side two-bedroom. He was living in a Chelsea sublet. Did she even consider where this dangerous rendezvous might lead?

"We're as good as divorced," he had written in one of their late night texts. "Just a lawyer away from being a free man in Paris." *Paris, Texas,* she snorted to herself. He claimed to be 51, which would make him more than ten years her senior. Was forty trophy wife age? she wondered. And since when did Nora aspire to become anyone's trophy, anyway?

She turned on Saturday Night Live for company. She didn't recognize the actors doing Evening Update. The woman wasn't very funny at all. And the man reading the news could have been Dan. Except Dan was much better.

When had she lost her patience for her adoring, sexy, infantile, Kevin Bacon-obsessed husband? What microscopic shift in their marital universe had turned his sweet mannerisms into cloying routines? Was it Dan's boyish enthusiasm, or her own crushing lack of hope that filled her with such doubt? When had her aspirations been ground down to such nondescript sawdust?

Dan still believed. That was the rub. He saw the break right around the corner. She had watched him just the other night typing madly away at the computer and then playing out each of the characters in the flickering darkness of their tiny apartment. Were she not so cynical about his business, it would have been endearing. He had just enough crumbs to keep himself nourished. Only they were feeding his dreams, not hers. And whose fault was that? She could hardly accuse him of not caring. The guy was a galumphing puppy dog when it came to her writing career, her craft, her brilliant prospects. If anything, he believed in her more than she believed in herself.

Nora flipped aimlessly through the pablum on TV. When her one and only *Vanity Fair* piece had come out, she had briefly allowed herself the fantasy that her career would take off. That she would become the important writer she had envisioned all her life. Where had the pages of *that* chapter gone? She had become so inured to any hope of salvation that she had risked everything for a phantom doctor with a sailboat and a laptop. While Dan rehearsed in their living room, she cheated wirelessly in bed, separated from her husband by a thin sheet of tenement drywall. While Dan was auditioning for stardom, she was auditioning for adulterer. And it seemed, she sighed, her break had come first.

- 23 -
CHUCK

The sergeant had given out no information beyond the address of the hospital. And that Missy was alive, he assumed. Because if not, wouldn't they be driving to the morgue? That was how it always worked on the police procedurals he had grown addicted to since his age of unemployment. *Law & Order*, *CSI: New York*, *CSI: Miami*. He savored their predictability in his otherwise amorphous life. Unlike his days, the nightly shows had a beginning, a middle and an end. A team of handsome colleagues sifted through the evidence. A list of suspects was cribbed together. And in the final reel, they always got the bad guy. Life should be so satisfying and predictable.

The headlights coming at him on the Turnpike danced and twinkled in a steady blinding stream. Chuck squinted in his rearview mirror. He hit the toggle to dim the glare. He checked his speedometer. 65 steady. Good. Considering how much he had to drink, he wasn't even sure how he was keeping the car on the road.

Paula stared ahead. What was she thinking? They had not spoken a word since leaving the garage on 78th Street. The silence was suffocating, like the echo chamber their lives had become. When had they had run out of things to say? They shared a bed, they shared the chores, they shared the remote control. It was a life devoid of life, a picture postcard gone awry.

A flashing red beacon appeared out of nowhere. Chuck tensed. Shit, how fast was he going? 67. Paula saw the lights of the police car, too.

"Chuck, pull over. Tell them what happened."

"I wasn't speeding."

"Well you must have been doing something," she snapped.

Yes, it was all his fault. The lost job. The futile interviews. The dwindling savings account and the constricting budget. Paula could barely mask her disdain with him. She should have married Hank – the investment banker she had dated right before they met. Okay, so the guy was dull as dirt and probably a lousy lay to boot. Still, he was a provider. Henry. Hank! At least she'd be riding out the recession in the front seat of a six-series BMW and an 8,000-square foot house in Short Hills, instead of limping along in their measly existence with the past-due notices piling up on the bench in the foyer.

The twirling red lights gained on him, and for a fleeting moment Chuck fantasized about stomping down on the accelerator, feeling the roar of the engine shifting into low gear, and hurtling them at breakneck speed as fast as he could maneuver, threading his way through the late night traffic. Could he possibly outrun a New Jersey State Trooper? Not that it mattered. The cop would already have his license on his dashboard computer, the entire profile: the two traffic stops, the unpaid parking tickets. The third refinance and the tax installment plan. The missed college payment, his rising LDL count, and the Google search record of his furtive porn forays. There was no escaping anything any more. He eased off the gas. No need to get Paula killed just because he was having a bad day. If that was Plan B, he had the industrial-sized vial of Ambien he'd been squirreling away for months. Sleep before pain. There was always a way out.

"Damnit Chuck, pull over." The police car was roaring up on their left, traffic dropping out of the lane to clear a path. Chuck stole a glance at his wife in the muted glow of the dashboard light. She'd put on weight. Hadn't they all? Even so, in profile – the dark curly hair and the cute hook of her nose – he saw the woman he married. He felt a surge of warmth, thinking back to a stolen weekend in Atlantic City. The kids were at camp and he and Paula hadn't been away all summer. On a whim he'd surprised her, saying pack a swimsuit and a cocktail dress. She laughed like he was kidding, until she realized he was not. They'd burned a path down the Garden State Parkway, valeting their car at the Harrah's Resort. Paula was skeptical about the whole affair, until she found herself on the winning end of a thousand-dollar run at a twenty-five dollar craps table. He had not seen her eyes glisten like that in years, drink in one hand and dice in the other, hitting mark after mark to a cheering throng. Her hair was pulled back, her dress cut low, and when they returned to their room, they had made love as the sun came up over the rolling surf of the Atlantic Ocean.

It was only a weekend. It seemed like a lifetime ago. Chuck reached out with one hand and put his palm on his wife's warm cheek. Her eyes opened wide, her mouth about to register protest as the shrill scream of the siren drew closer.

- 24 -
PAULA

Guarded condition. That was all she could get out of the ER desk at Summit General. Guarded from what? The randomness of teenage excess that challenged their fragile lives every time they stepped out the door? Good luck with that, Paula thought.

Her one and only job had been to protect her daughter and at that she had failed. When Missy and Tom were little more than toddlers and Chuck's career was clear sailing under blue skies, she had relinquished her own Wall Street trajectory without a whisper of regret. She had sunk into her role as the mother of two young children like a trapeze artist tumbling into the net. It was her single most important choice and she had not vacillated. What comforts they had, seemed her due. The spacious house, the decent schools. The tree-lined streets and the quaint village square. She took it all for granted. The kids. Chuck. The fluffy snow globe life that he provided. Even recently, as the wheels came off, she had tried to look the other way. That was his problem to solve, not hers. But now this.

She had seen the red lights coming up from behind them first. *Pull over Chuck.* She never should have allowed Missy to get in that car with her friends. They weren't old enough to drive. They cranked tunes and hung out the windows. They texted. They drank and smoked and broke curfew in the guarded climes of their pristine community. And yet she had nonchalantly allowed her daughter to travel the length of the Garden State Parkway with a gaggle of teens. How could she expect them to navigate the vast array of split second decisions required to guide a seven-thousand-pound car hurtling down the road.

The police car gained on them, but Chuck did not slow down. Paula tried to fight back the tears. She had abrogated the one adult responsibility she was tasked with, and for what. To wile away the night with a bunch of citified friends who drank too much and preened themselves on art and politics and goddamned food – as if a hunk of expensive beef could cure the world's ills? She should have driven the girls to the cheerleading trials herself. That was her role. They were kids for Chrissakes. So what if she was un-cool and wore size 8 jeans and had no idea who Jay-Z was. That was the Mommy's job, to be professionally dull and un-hip and guarantee safe passage to the middle years, or at the very least, get them out of high school and into an environment where they had a chance to grow up.

She looked down at her hand. She was clutching her cell phone so tightly that she was surprised it had not cracked open like a husk. She had called the Emergency Room three times so far. "We have no further information."

The muffled roar of the engine enveloped them like a coffin. Was Chuck planning to outrace a New Jersey State trooper? She wondered how he was even keeping the car on the road. *Just pull over. Let them deliver us from this nightmare.* How could she blame him? He had been the one to challenge Missy's trip to Trenton that morning. Not her. And when Missy had called just a few hours ago to ask if she could spend the night with friends, it had been Chuck who said no at first blush. *Daddy's little girl.* Everyone at Lucy's had made fun of his antiquated ways. Even she had mocked his over-protectiveness. He did not deserve it. For what was he really but a stuffed teddy bear with an unlimited cache of love for his family and an extended run of bad luck.

Your daughter is lying broken in pieces in a New Jersey hospital.

God she was a horrible person. A horrible person and a horrible mom. She had failed them all. *Just don't let it be worse than it already is,* she prayed. I will learn to change. I will live with myself, but make this be okay.

She wanted to scream and climb over Chuck and jam her foot on the brake pedal. *Please, please stop the car and let me out.* What was he doing? They were floating down the New Jersey Turnpike in the middle of the night, the wine and pot throbbing at her temples, and all she knew was Chuck's tender touch on her cheek, a tragic glimmer in his brooding eyes.

"Have fun in the city, Mom and Dad. Luv ya!"

She cannot be gone.

Paula tried to stop mentally thumbing through the bible of second chances. Let the cop cuff them both and throw away the key. After. Not now. The spinning beacon filled the car with a blinding splash of phosphorus red. Then, without slowing, the trooper blew by, disappearing into the sea of taillights as fast as he had appeared.

- 25 -

DAN

He stared in earnest at her breasts. Her elbows rested on the bar as she tapped out a text on her iPhone. Dan liked her. She had short dark hair, hole-y Levis, a white t-shirt, and scuffed cowboy boots. She projected just a little butch. Very sexy. He wondered who she was texting. Maybe she was checking her Match.com. Wasn't everybody?

The woman looked his way. Busted. He returned his gaze to his beer. As if that was what he needed. It was hardly making a dent, but at least he was maintaining. The mere thought of sobriety was more than he could handle.

Dan was enveloped with a profound sense of disbelief. Divorce was not a currency he traded in. None of his friends had been through it. That was unless he counted Nicole, and she was really Lucy's friend. He had felt badly when Nicole and Bill split up, but while Lucy was bemoaning the fate of their kids, he found himself mainly wondering if Nic was a good lay. He stole another glance at the woman at the bar. Was *she*? Christ, was he really thinking about divorce? A handful of hours ago he was happily humping his beautiful wife against the slicked-up glass of their shower door.

He quaffed his dwindling stout and set it down on the bar with a thump. He drummed his fingers nervously against the pint glass. He might have to take a leak before the next round.

"I hope you're as sexy in person as you are in prose." The words of the email would not go away. He wracked his brain in search of what he had done wrong. Sure, money had been tight, but they got by. He cooked, he cleaned, he did all the chores. He always told Nora that if things got too desperate he'd go back to work. Besides, she had been supportive of his career move. She had helped him pick his new headshots and even admitted that he looked younger than a lot of the ingénues out there working. Certainly younger than Kevin Bacon. It did not add up. His writing was cranking along. His agent was enthusiastic. Nora's job at the magazine was secure. Their love life was better than ever. Or so he thought. Had it all been a ruse? What if she had been faking her orgasms? God, anything but that.

The woman at the bar slipped her iPhone into her jeans pocket. Dan gawked at her. She was young, maybe thirty – a decade too early for him to even consider. Damn she had nice tits. He felt so confused.

She nodded his way. Their eyes met and she flashed a sweet sympathetic smile. Two strangers at the local on a Saturday night. Dan hadn't played this role in a long time. He obscured his ring finger beneath the bar.

Oh my god you are so funny. No, c'mon over. My roommate's out of town. Boston. Philly. I don't know. I hope Lite beer is okay.

He hadn't seen the inside of a New York studio apartment since the previous millennium. Good lord, there was an ashtray.

You get high? She cupped his hand as he lit the joint for her. What was that music? Joni Mitchell meets Lady Gaga? What did he know. Or care.

So you're divorced?

Well, we're kind of separated.

Whatever.

He felt the breath sucking out of him as they kissed on her second-hand sofa. How could something he did so often with one person feel so different with another? He reached under her t-shirt. She stopped him and peeled it off without a thought. His jaw dropped. *Are you always this bold?*

Don't talk. Just kiss me. She ran her hand across the bulge in his jeans. She stopped at his pocket and slipped her hand in. She pulled his wedding ring out on her pinky finger. She waved it playfully in front of him.

I can explain.

You don't have to. She straddled him, unsnapping her bra. *Just don't speak. It's better that way.*

"Last call, pal."

Dan snapped to. Cute Butch Woman shuffled some bills onto the bar and got up to leave. Dan followed her with his eyes as she walked to the door, gazing at her receding boots and bobbing head. She had a great ass. His wife had a great ass. Dan did not need any more asses. He felt the oncoming flutter of a panic attack. This was so off script. What the hell was he going to do?

- 26 -

NICOLE AND GRAY

"That was inspired, my dear."

"Mmmmm." Nicole lay with her head on Gray's chest, her hand caressing his receding cock. It was a nice penis, just perfect. Not gargantuan, but certainly a member any man would be proud of. Did it live up to the rumor mill of black cockdom? It wasn't like she had a yardstick by which to compare. Gray was her first in that department, and he filled her with a pleasure that was almost embarrassing. Apparently the feelings were mutual.

She and Bill had never engaged in white-hot kiss and make-up sex because Bill, to the best of his knowledge, was never wrong. Therefore, there was never anything to fight about. It was maddening to say the least.

Gray had barely said a word in the cab back to the hotel. Nicole knew he was steamed, but she was not aware how much so. In the six months they'd been together, they had not had a major blowout. Gray tended to simmer when he had something on his mind, like he was preparing a lecture, or contemplating an interesting research paper. She was unprepared for his anger and when it came, it was surprising in its fury, like an unexpected summer thunderstorm. They had exited the taxi and walked calmly through the hotel lobby. They rode up in the elevator in silence. And then once they were behind closed doors, he came undone. Yes, she was out of line. Yes, she was stoned and drunk. Yes, she called him out and made a fool of him in front of the whole gang. Isn't that what friends were for?

When Gray was done with his tirade – and when she had made her requisite counter-arguments and stomped her foot petulantly enough to be heard two floors below – their fight went up in smoke and a trail of scattered clothes. Cheating on Bill, while of questionable moral fiber, had unleashed in Nicole a side she had all but forgotten. Hers and Gray's midtown hotel faced out on an opposing apartment building. If the thick windows were not one-way glass, a good portion of East 56th Street was treated to quite a show. Good for them, Nicole smiled to herself.

"Honey, how do you do that to me?" Gray groaned.

"What? Ohhh, that!" Deep in thought, Nicole was still stroking him and amazingly, he had grown hard again. "Wow," she said with true admiration. "You really are my rock star."

"And you are my insatiable nymphet."

Nicole unhanded him, burrowing in closer, needing to feel his presence, the smell of his skin, the warmth of his breath on her neck.

"I'm sorry, Gray."

"For what?" he asked, surprised.

"For outing you."

"I think they noticed I was black."

"Very funny. I mean blathering on about your not wanting to come to the party and all."

"Oh please, who cares. You laid it out there. You said a lot of things nobody wanted to hear. Very brave of you dear."

"Thanks," she said. "I suppose our invite to Paula's next

do might not be forthcoming any time soon."

"You were a little harsh."

"But she was so all over me from the gitgo with her prissy little Republican June Cleaver napkin-wringing PTA conservatism. Ughhh, I am so not cut out for the 'burbs." She sighed. "God I hope Missy's okay." She was pissed off, but not inhumane.

"Yes. It's too awful to even think about."

Nicole ran one finger across Gray's chest, doodling as she stared at the ceiling. "Do you think we should get married?"

"What?" An ice bath would have had less effect on his turgid member.

"Ju-u-u-st kidding," she said. "Sorry." She turned her head away on the pillow.

"Where the heck did *that* come from?"

"I don't know. Thinking about Nora and Dan I guess."

"They're hardly a role model," Gray said, a little confused.

"They used to be," Nicole said. "They were always so playful together. And Nora is brilliant and clever and she's a poet and she dresses great. And Dan is always getting roles in these wacky avant-garde plays. They have edge, you know? Like a really good jazz duet."

"That's one way to put it," Gray said.

"I suppose you never really know what's going on behind people's bedroom doors."

"At least not for nine and a half years."

"Hunhhh? Why nine and a half years?"

"Statistics. Fifty-two percent of marriages that fail, tend to do so just short of the tenth anniversary."

Nicole ruminated on this. Her boyfriend was, if nothing else, a fount of useless information. "How long have we been together?" she asked at last.

"Six months."

"Really?"

"We met on April 20th. The day I went on your show."

"You remember our anniversary. That is so sweet."

"You want flowers?"

"Diamonds and rubies."

"I'm a professor."

"Fair enough. Flowers will do." She rolled over and kissed him on the lips. "And that bit about getting married? Just pretend I never said anything."

"Excuse me?" He propped himself up on one elbow and stared at her with raised eyebrow.

"If you ever have any interest in walking down the aisle with me, feel free to bring it up *after* our tenth anniversary. Not a day sooner." Nicole nestled deep into Gray's arms and closed her eyes. Sometimes, she thought, as exhaustion crashed over her like a wave, the moment was the best place to be.

- 27 -
CHUCK AND PAULA

They were out of the car before the sound of the Honda's engine had even subsided. Two boxy, square ambulances sat next to the Emergency Room parking bay. Paula couldn't help but crane her neck and peer in. Chuck took her arm, shepherding her into the hospital through the sliding glass doors that read *Visitors*. The fluorescent light hit them like an X-ray. They were in a wide foyer. Paula shook loose from Chuck's grasp and placed herself in front of the information desk.

"Melissa Dempster?" she asked, as Chuck came up by her side. His wife's face was drawn and pale, her voice squeezed and tight as if it were funneling through a straw.

"When was she brought in?" the nurse asked.

"We got a call from the police about two hours ago." Paula hung her head with shame. "We were in the city," she said in a whisper.

"Here we go," the nurse said.

"Is she okay?"

"Come with me."

Paula followed, the clicking of her dress heels conspicuous and out of place in the antiseptic hallway. Chuck was a half step behind. The nurse's voice gave away nothing.

He felt short of breath. The proximity to crisis was crushing the air right out of him.

They turned a corner. His heart froze. A policeman sat on a bench outside a room. It was worse than anything he could ever have imagined.

"These are the Dempsters," the nurse said. The officer stood up.

"Officer Russ Grimsley. I'm a sergeant with the Summit Township Police."

Chuck extended a hand and for one crazy second he felt like he was on a job interview.

"Officer," Paula said, an uncanny calm to her voice, as if every last mother's defense mechanism had kicked in. A cloudburst of laughter spilled from the room. Followed by giggles. And then more laughter. Paula slumped against her husband.

"Ma'am?" The officer took her arm, just in case she was about to faint dead away.

"Missy," Paula said, her last vestige of control crumpling.

"She's okay," the officer said.

Chuck took a deep breath. Gulping, he tried to compose himself.

"Let me see her," Paula said.

Another hysterical peal of laughter burst from the room. The officer blocked the way.

"I want to see her now!"

"Yes, but she's under observation. And I need to tell you, when the doctors release her, she's going to be arrested."

"What?"

"Oh my god, may we pleeeease order some pizza?"

Paula's eyes widened. Something came over Chuck – it resembled a smile – his body released from the death grip it had been in since his cell phone had rung back in the city. He went from the abyss to reborn in a nanosecond, the plot revealed. Paula still looked ashen.

"Arrested? What in God's name are you talking about?"

"She's baked!" Chuck said, trying not to laugh out loud. As far as he was concerned, it was time to start handing out the cigars.

"What?" Paula said.

"High as a kite."

"Correct," Officer Grimsley nodded. "That would be an appropriate description."

"Why is she here?" Paula demanded.

"It's the law. We can't take her to the station house until the effects of the drugs wear off. Also, she injured her ankle. I'm not sure what the results of the X-rays were."

"My daughter does not take drugs," Paula announced.

More peals of laughter rang out from the examining room. Missy was not alone.

"What's she on?" Chuck asked, relieved to have been granted his one wish of still being the father of a teenage girl.

"We're waiting on the tox screen results," the nurse said, at last getting a chance to assert her authority. "But my guess is a combination of marijuana and probably more than a little cranberry-flavored vodka."

"She's—." Paula was still having trouble registering the information.

"Drunk and stoned." Chuck finished the sentence for her. And then under his breath, added, "Go figure." It was hard to imagine that the apple had fallen far.

"Who's in there with her?' Paula asked.

"I'm not at liberty to say, ma'am."

"Sounds like Carla and Patty to me, don't you think?" Chuck said. Paula was not quite at the place where she could have a sense of humor about this yet.

"Come on," the nurse said, giving in. "You can see her for a minute." She led Paula by the arm. Chuck stayed behind, waiting until his wife was out of earshot.

"What are the charges, Officer?" he asked.

"Possession of a Grade 3 non-felony drug. Possession of alcohol by a minor. Non-felony disturbing the peace. Non-felony public lewdness."

"They weren't driving?"

"No sir. There were no cars involved. Thank God."

"Thank God."

The cop all of a sudden became human to Chuck. He wondered if he had kids. Chuck was already micromanaging the next steps of this nightmare turned logistical. "Where did you pick them up?" he asked.

"In the fountain in the middle of the village."

Chuck took it all in. Stoned and drunk in a sleepy New Jersey town. How familiar. It was exactly how Chuck and his friends had spent the better part of their high school career.

"Wait," he said, a thought occurring to him. "Did you say public lewdness?"

"Yes sir."

"What were they doing?"

Officer Grimsley stared down at his feet. He looked like a college kid who'd gotten busted on a date with the professor's daughter.

"They were, uhhh, displaying their private parts in a flagrant manner that violates the village's bylaws."

"What?" Chuck asked, incredulous.

"They were skinny dipping, sir." Officer Grimsley picked at a spot of lint on the arm of his uniform. The nurse came out of the examining room with her clipboard.

"You can go in, sir."

"Thanks," Chuck said. "In a moment." He waited for

the nurse to pad back to her station. Then he confronted the policeman.

"Can we talk?" Chuck asked.

"Yes," Officer Grimsley replied.

"Away from this room?" The men walked down the hall to the snack machines.

"That's a long list of charges against my daughter, Officer."

"Yes sir. It was a busy night."

"Missy has never been in trouble with the law in her life."

"I know. I've already run her."

"She's an A student. She's doing dance this fall, and she's a midfielder on the soccer team. She's not very good," Chuck admitted.

"Still nice to play a sport," Officer Grimsley said.

"Yes," Chuck agreed. "She's thinking about Penn or Wisconsin, but money, you know? Rutgers may be the best we can do. And frankly, I'd be darned proud if she went there."

"I'm third year criminal law at Rutgers night school, sir."

The two men looked at each other. Chuck was starting to feel like a bit player on one of his habitual TV shows.

"Can you tell me how this works, Officer?"

"We haven't done our paperwork yet. We carted them over here in the squad. An ambulance wasn't necessary."

"So they haven't been formally arrested?"

"They've been read their rights. Charges will be filed in the morning." Chuck and Officer Grimsley's eyes met. He seemed bright and ambitious, Chuck thought. The kind of guy he could see Missy dating in college.

"You guys have a jail over there at the station house?"

"A small holding cell."

"Pretty unhappy place for a high school kid to find herself in, don't you think?"

"Extremely." The men nodded in agreement.

"Officer? Would you believe me if I told you this is the first time I even knew that my daughter drinks, much less gets high?"

The officer subtly appraised Chuck, taking in his bloodshot eyes, the rumpled blazer, the shoes in need of replacing. "I would. And if I'm any judge of character, I'd guess that other than her court appearance, I'll probably never see her again."

"Except perhaps at Rutgers."

Officer Grimsley smiled. "That would be an unusual reunion."

Chuck looked at his watch. "Good God, it's four in the morning. Can I buy you a cup of coffee?"

"Thanks, but I can't accept that."

"Of course not." What was he thinking, attempting to bribe a cop. "Well, I better go rescue my wife. They may have to put *her* under observation after tonight." Chuck thought he detected a trace of a smile on Officer Grimsley's face. He turned to walk away.

"Mr. Dempster?"

Chuck stopped and faced the officer.

"Let your wife know that disturbing the peace and public lewdness are both level three misdemeanors. No record. No time. No different than a parking ticket."

"I will. And the possession charge?"

The officer looked at his watch. "I may have lost the evidence out by the park. In which case there's no reason to even put that in my report. You know?"

"I do," Chuck said. Officer Grimsley reached into the pocket next to his gun and dug out some change for the coffee machine. Chuck walked back down the hallway to go reclaim his family.

- 28 -
LIONEL

Lucy awoke with a start on the leather sofa. It was still nighttime. Street light permeated the darkened apartment. The stereo was still on, its cobalt blue power dial illuminated. Groggy, she rose and switched it off. *Huhhh?* She must have been half-awake. Music continued to resonate in her head. It took a moment. Then she realized. The notes were coming from the study.

She padded in her bare feet across the apartment. That's weird, she thought. Lionel had closed the door. He never locked himself in. She pushed it ajar. The room was dark. She could make out his silhouette, sitting on the piano bench. His frame was firm and upright, but for his shoulders, which swayed like marsh grass in a tide, his great head dipping with the flow of his arms as he played. She stood transfixed. Nothing like this had sprung from Lionel in months. She held her breath. The music stopped. He looked up.

"It's beyond beautiful," Lucy said.

He did not speak. Lucy could see his hands on the keyboard. He had such lovely pianist fingers. She was so drawn to them, even to this day. She waited with anticipation, until she realized, in fact, he was done. He slumped on the bench.

"Is something wrong, Lionel?"

He turned his head and peered out the picture window. He looked like a bust of Beethoven, she thought, backlit against the dim city lights. Her eyes grew accustomed to the dark. Then she saw it. Sitting on his leather chair. An embroidered ancient valise. Hers. From the deepest recesses of her closet. Its scuffed gold clasps were snapped open, the bag's neatly packed contents clearly visible. She drew a sharp breath. Lionel turned at the sound.

"Were you going to tell me, or just be gone?" he asked.

She didn't know whether to laugh or cry. Lionel stared at her, his lips quivering, an indescribable look of pain on his face. This marriage thing, it was not some college prank. When had they all become such grownups, she wondered.

The old relic of an overnight bag had lived in the depths of her spacious walk-in closet for longer than she could remember. It rested beneath the stacks of storage containers and computer cartons and damaged luggage that they had not hauled out for years. Lucy had nearly forgotten about it. Her mother had given it to her eons ago, when they decided to sell the house in Greenburgh, after Ruth's latest fall made it evident that she could not maintain the home any longer. They had been sitting in Lucy's childhood bedroom, reminiscing, when Ruth pulled the valise out. She'd kept this very same suitcase, she confided, packed and hidden away, untouched for forty years. In it, she always had a change of clothes, toiletries, and twenty dollars socked away.

"*You never know when you might need it,*" Ruth had told her in a pragmatic tone of voice. So together, mother and daughter rummaged through Lucy's closet, filling the bag with some of her most cherished clothes from her college days: a Brown sweatshirt, a pair of bell bottom jeans, a tattered flannel shirt. At the time it was nothing more than a joke. A nostalgic goof. A goof that had found its way into the recesses of Lucy's New York apartment, all but forgotten by her.

Lucy gazed at Lionel. She could only imagine what was going on in his tortured mind. Her mother's generation had insured themselves against the vagaries of marriage with clutched mad money in a purse. Or a packed valise in an attic. Lucy's slept with a stranger at a broadcast convention. Or surfed the Internet for a zipless fuck. Another great boon for technology, she thought.

"Lionel, let's just go to bed," she said. "We can talk about this in the morning."

"I followed you last week."

"You what?" Her brain raced, the damning words sinking in.

"You said you were going to the gym. I was trying to write, but I couldn't stand another minute alone in this infernal prison. So I tried to catch up with you. For a coffee. Or drinks. Anything. I didn't want to be alone."

"You could have stopped me."

"You were too far ahead. I chased you down 79th Street, but when you got to the gym, you didn't go in. You turned right. So I followed you. To the subway station. To the uptown Number 6 local. I watched the doors close. When the train pulled out, you were gone."

What a mess, Lucy thought to herself. "Where did you think I was going?"

"Not the gym, that's for sure." He stared at her. "That internist of yours is uptown."

Oh my lord, did someone put absinthe in the wine? Dr. Guttman of all people. The man was hallucinating. Or certifiable. Or both! She noticed that Lionel still had a whisky going. The ice was fresh. He'd all but been on a Lagavulin I.V. for the past eight hours. He was over the edge.

"Why didn't you just call me?"

"Brilliant idea," Lionel chuckled. "*Hi. You've reached Lucy. I'm out fucking my doctor. Please leave a message and I'll get back to you as soon as I can.*"

"Is that what you think?" she asked in a cold voice. "Is that really what you think of me?"

"You don't want to know."

"You're goddamned right I don't." She felt the bile rising in her. She'd just about had her fill. The years of suspicion. The barely muted accusations. Maybe she *should* have slept with her internist. If you're going to pay the price, you might as well do the crime.

"There's more," Lionel said.

"Spare me."

"I tried to break into your email."

"You didn't."

"I did. I tried every bloody password I could think of."

"You bastard."

"Then I ripped through every last one of your American Express bills."

So that was the reclamation project he had been working on in the study. Her private life had been strafed. "And what did you find?"

"Nothing."

Go figure. She stared at him with a contempt that she did not know she had in her.

"Where were you going?" Lionel asked.

"Kitchen Arts & Letters. On Lex and 94th. The cookbook store." It was the first convenient fiction that came to mind. And why not? Did it really matter what she said?

"Kitchen Arts & Letters?" He stared back with pure disgust. "At least have the decency to concoct a digestible lie."

Lucy looked at him, helpless to stanch the bleeding.

Everyone had secrets. Maybe Lionel did too. She was too tired to give a damn.

"Believe whatever you want. Okay?"

Lionel turned from her and closed the lid to the piano. He ran his fingers across its polished surface. He had created something this evening. Maybe more than he bargained for. At least his work was done. He could move on.

"Nice dinner, Luce," he said. The sarcasm dripped like honey.

"Thanks a lot," she replied. She didn't know if she wanted to kill him or institutionalize him.

"Don't mention it."

Lionel walked over to the chair where the old valise lay. He thumbed through it for a moment, examining its contents. "Hmmm." He gently closed the leather lid. The sound of the clasps snapping shut clicked like a loaded gun. He left the valise on the chair, picked up his whisky tumbler, and walked out the door.

Part Four
The Morning After

- 29 -
NORA

The clatter of the deadbolt startled her awake.

She had slept alone.

The light of dawn invaded her window. She propped herself up on one elbow, adrift in their queen-sized bed. Shit, her head was killing her. She walked into the bathroom and downed a huge glass of water and two Advil. Then she walked out of the bedroom to explore.

The apartment was empty. A comforter was strewn across the couch where Dan had encamped for the night. An empty, crumb-covered plate sat on the coffee table. Now it was coming back to her. The last thing she heard before passing out was the sound of Dan stomping in at two in the morning and raiding the fridge. She could tell by the racket that he was sloshed. She heard the American cheese being opened, the rustle of the bread package, and then the sound of the whirring microwave. *Hebrew National hot dog on white bread with runny melted cheese. Perfect hangover prevention food.* That was what he used to say when they'd both come home drunk together from their local pub, so many years ago. What was cute back then.

The sight of his sloppy nest by the couch made her sad. They had always managed to find their way back to bed after one of their disagreements. Dan was nowhere to be seen. The chains of his elaborate bicycle storage pulley system hung empty. She was not surprised. He often rode at daybreak. He said it was the purest time of day to clear his head and think big thoughts. No doubt he had some real doozies knocking about this morning.

She glanced out past the rusted fire escape and down to the street. The sky was barely light over Amsterdam Avenue. Not a soul in sight. How could you want someone to be there and not be there at the same time? Did familiarity breed contempt for all couples? Or was it a New York thing, where people lived in such close quarters that every fart, itch and belch was shared. Maybe that was why marriage in the city was such a tenuous proposition. Mating humans were simply not intended to live in shoeboxes. There just was not enough space to run and hide.

She wandered over to her desk and keyed the computer to life, more out of force of habit than anything else. She wondered if Greg was popping out of bed and checking his email, too. Maybe he was on tenterhooks hoping for a response from her, even before he enjoyed his first cup of coffee. She sighed. What had started out as a bored stunt had exploded beneath hers and Dan's fragile existence. If she tugged on this thread any further, it would unravel everything. How long does it take to unspool sixteen years, she wondered.

She opened her browser and logged on to Match.com. She had no new messages. She opened Greg's email again and stared at his number. She thought about picking up the phone and dialing. How would he feel about receiving a call at this ungodly hour? Maybe one of his conquests was curled up in his arms right now. He probably had dozens of suitors. She might just be one more online psycho bitch looking to hook up. What did she know of this crazy game?

She scrolled through The Collected Works of Dr. Greg. Their meaning had faded overnight, leaving them flat and flavorless like a leftover glass of champagne. The only thing to be salvaged was couched in the last pixilated image beneath his name. Ten digits that could rock her world. She clicked the box next to the delete icon and entered a *check* symbol. Then, on a whim, she grabbed a pen and a lime green post-it pad that she kept in a tray on her desk. She scrawled down his phone number and tore the post-it off. She folded it in half, and then in half again, balling it up as tight as a wad of chewing gum. She opened her desk drawer and shoved the piece of paper back as far as it would go, lost in the dust and pushpins and taxi receipts and gnawed-down pencils and paper clips. No name. No identification. Just a number. Were Dan to ever happen upon it, the folded post-it would be meaningless. A long ago reminder stuffed away with so many other unfinished projects, buried in the back of a drawer.

She hit delete on Greg's message. Then she navigated her way to the Member Services page of the website. In the space of a few short clicks, she removed her profile and canceled her account, exorcising herself from the files of Match.com. She wandered into the kitchen to start some coffee. She wondered when Dan would be home.

- 30 -
PAULA

The old Honda glided down their cul-de-sac and bumped over the lip of the driveway. The neighborhood was as still as a pond. The electric garage door jerked open. Chuck braked to a stop his usual quarter inch away from the pegboard athletic wall he had built when the children were young. Balls and racquets and lacrosse sticks and cross country skis stuck out in every which direction, monument to their kids' suburban youth. *Both* kids, Paula thought, with something far deeper than relief. Chuck sat in the driver's seat, his hands still clutching the wheel.

"Honey, the engine?" He did not move. "Chuck, can you turn the engine off please?"

"Right. Sorry." He snapped the key. The absence of sound was startling. Sunday morning. Daybreak. They were home. He hit the garage remote. The door creaked back down.

"Are you coming in?" Paula asked.

"In a second."

"Are you okay?"

"I am. I just need to sit here for a moment. Decompress, you know?"

"Okay. I've got to use the bathroom."

"Yep."

Her door closed with a muffled slam. She walked around the back of the car and let herself in through the utility room.

She blinked in the milky light of the front hallway, trapped between night and day. She drank in the silence. The house was immaculate. The carpet threads had been vacuumed so vigorously that they were nearly standing on end. The signal on their burglar alarm glowed a harmless green. They hadn't armed it in years. What was there to steal? She set her bag on the settee by the window, like a stranger in her own home. She sat down and pulled off her pumps. *Blessed relief.* She kneaded the balls of her feet and felt the tension draining out of her. Her daughter was in jail. She was alive. It was an odd juxtaposition. A wonderful problem to have. She would deal, later.

Paula walked into the bathroom on the ground floor and sat on the toilet for a long time, even after she was done. The guest towels were embroidered with blue and white ducks that matched the untouched waxy little balls of perfumed soap. How tacky. What could she have been thinking? They had not entertained in ages.

She walked out of the bathroom. The carpeting felt good on her bare feet. She rummaged through her purse until she found her cell phone. No messages. She stared at the screen thoughtfully. She'd call Lucy in a moment. First she had some business to attend to. She punched up Nicole's number and started to type a text. She really had gone off on her. She wondered how much of it was the pot talking. Still. She composed a brief note about Missy. Then, as an afterthought, she added one last line. "Really liked Gray. Happy for you. xoxo." She signed off.

Exhaustion settled over her like fog. Their neatly made bed sounded perfect. She took one step up the landing before she realized the house was too quiet.

"Chuck?"

Nothing.

She walked back down the stairs and around to the kitchen. He was nowhere to be seen. She had a bad thought. She hurried through the utility room door and burst into the garage. The smell of the engine's exhaust hit her. They'd been meaning to have the old Honda's muffler repaired for months. It was an expense Chuck said could wait. She shielded her eyes and peered into the driver side window. The car was empty. She hit the garage opener switch on the wall. The creaking door tilted slowly up to the daylight, letting the remnants of exhaust escape into the morning air.

She stepped outside and stood with her hands on her hips beneath the basketball hoop that Chuck and Tommy had sunk into a dozen sacks of Redi-Mix concrete, years ago. Her boys still liked to play pickup games whenever Tommy came home from college. Where had her husband gone?

She walked across the lawn to the front door of the house. It was still locked from the inside. For the second time since the interminable evening had begun, she felt a flicker of panic in her chest. She hurried past the empty planters and followed the chipped flagstone path around to the back yard. There. She let out a relieved sigh.

Chuck sat on the wrought iron love bench they had installed by the tomato garden, his back to her, elbows on his knees. They had not planted this year. The patch was weedy and overgrown. "Chuck?"

She sat down next to him. He turned toward her. His cheeks were streaked with tears, his eyes rimmed red and full.

"Oh sweetie." She engulfed him in her arms. His entire body began to shake.

"I'm sorry," he said through his sobs.

"For what?"

"Everything." His face squinched up in anguish.

She pulled his head to her breast. "It's okay my love. *She's* okay. You can let it go. I'm here. We'll get through this together. All of it. I promise."

Chuck sat up and gazed at his wife. How many times are you lucky enough to get a do-over, he wondered. It was so out of his control. He wanted to spill it all, give up his secrets, open the books – let Paula in like he had never done before. He tried to compose himself, but it was too soon. He crumpled back into her arms.

She idly stroked his hair. Dew glistened on the grass in the growing morning light. They had stopped paying the landscaping service in July. Maybe she'd mow the lawn later. It was a start. She had raised a family and they had turned out fine. She was good at this. Maybe the job description was changing, but that was all right. She wouldn't be the first mother who had to make an unexpected return to the workplace. She might have to dust off a few old skills to get back on course, but it was what she wanted. Her family. Her home. Safe. Together. Whatever it took. She was ready.

- 31 -
DAN

Upper Broadway was as quiet and empty as a Nebraska plain. Dan pedaled down the middle of the avenue, the gears of his Schwinn 10-speed clicking. At 96th Street, he turned right and coasted down the steep hill until he hit the Hudson River bike path. He pulled up to a rusting side rail at the geographical edge of the island of Manhattan, mere feet away from the swirling waters. He was alone. He stared into the swift current. He could tumble over and let the river wash his troubles away. In San Francisco, the Golden Gate Bridge had elaborate suicide nets installed to prevent depressed artists like him from doing just that. In New York, the only physical barrier between a contemplative thespian and a watery grave was a trail of strewn beer cans and a lone bored pigeon.

He pushed off from the railing, set the bike into fifth gear, and started pedaling south down the path. No way did his story end with that tired cliché.

The overcaffeinated, velocipede enthusiasts were out now. Pseudo-cyclists on thousand dollar Shimanos, Bianchis, Cannondales – clubs of men in spandex jerseys emblazoned with phony sponsorships for imagined races they had never attempted. Dan's Dead t-shirt rippled in the wind. He was starting to break a good sweat.

At the 23rd Street Pier, he passed a dawn yoga class. Several dozen people stretched and straddled and downward-dogged into the morning sun, glinting off the river. He bumped through what little remained of the original Meatpacking District beneath the elevated tracks of the over-hyped High Line. Below Spring Street, One World Trade rose like the phoenix. How he missed the boxy landmarks that once dominated the city view from every conceivable angle. Whenever he and Nora had found themselves lost in the warren-like streets of the Village, they need only locate the lights of the towers to get their bearings. He had courted her downtown, their romance blossoming long before the days of 9/11. They were starving artists – the actor and the writer – cheap wine in one hand, smokes in the other, bodies pressed close at The Lion's Head Pub. She was everything he'd ever wanted. He pedaled harder.

At the tip of the island, he circled Battery Park and slowed to salute Lady Liberty. A Staten Island Ferry was cutting through the hanging mist of New York Harbor. He wove through the empty canyons of the financial district, then navigated his way over the cobblestones of Fulton Street. In Chinatown, the streets were growing crowded. Old Chinese men were unloading buckets of clams and scallops from panel trucks. A wooden crate of live frogs dripped black water. Fresh frog legs would be on the menu somewhere tonight. Dan wondered when the frogs became *not* live.

He crossed Canal and picked his way through Little Italy. He could chart the change of neighborhoods by scent alone. The aroma of fresh bread and sweet pastry filled his nostrils as he bounced over Crosby Street through Soho. God it was good to be alive in New York. Even if your agent sucked and you really hadn't had a good audition in months and your wife was banging some asshole named Greg.

He pedaled hard up Third Avenue. At 42nd Street he saw he was going to miss the light. He charged into the intersection like a deranged bike messenger, swerving around a bus and nearly going head-to-head with a black Suburban SUV. Miraculously, he avoided a collision and swung back into his lane. A bracing "Fuck you asshole" rang out from behind him as he continued uptown.

He entered the Park at 60th and ascended the horse carriage path. He hit the 72nd Street traverse and swooped down low and hard. He passed the Metropolitan Museum of Art, pedaling with all his might. He tucked into the rich ripe curves blazing down the Big Hill and whizzed past the pool at 110th Street. It was half-drained for fall, its aquamarine walls exposed to the world. Now he was a man on a mission. Going up the flip side of the hill, his muscles were screaming, gears whirring. He raced past the flashing yellow light at the summit, letting out a war whoop as he flew over the crest. He lifted both arms triumphantly like pre-steroids Lance Armstrong beneath the Arc de Triomphe. Success. He'd traversed the entire city before the sun had hit the skyscrapers on Central Park South. Harlem to the tip of Manhattan, Chinatown to the Upper West Side.

He pulled up to his apartment and dismounted, drenched in sweat and gulping for air. Fuck his wife and the poet stranger. He'd take a stand before she fucked him. He unlocked the front door and lit into the stairs. Five flights up – with bicycle. He arrived at the top landing. He slipped the key in the front door and pushed it open. Nora looked up from her computer.

"Hey," he said, deflating as quickly as a tire crunching through glass.

"Hey," she said. He stood staring at the monitor screen behind her. Whatever grandiose strategy he had crafted over the course of his ride, flickered. At least there was no need for her to surreptitiously log out. He knew that drill. Nora did not move.

"Go right ahead," Dan said. "It's not like it's a secret any more."

"There's nothing to hide," she replied, making no attempt to cover the evidence.

"I'm sure. Lucy knows. Nicole knows. It's probably on Facebook by now. My mother knows. My brother knows. My goddamned agent's probably reading about it over her morning macchiato."

"That's right Dan. Make it all about you. Again. As always."

"Me? How's this about me? Aren't *you* the one handing out your cell phone number to some pervy banker who thinks you write like Annie Proulx?"

"He happens to be a doctor."

"Well there you go. I feel so much better."

"Maybe if you spent five lousy minutes thinking about someone other than yourself, I wouldn't be sitting home alone at nights surfing the Web."

"Oh for Chrissakes Nora, you're my wife. Who do you think I'm thinking about? I make the bed. I do the laundry. I buy the groceries. Who the hell do you think I'm doing all that for?"

"I'm not talking about running to Fairway to buy twelve-packs of freaking Ramen, Dan. Do you ever give a moment's thought to how *I* feel? Do you think I enjoy bringing home the bacon for both of us year after year? You think it's fun schlepping down to that shithole of an office they call a magazine and writing about software deals? You don't think there's something else beating in here?" She pounded her breastbone with her fist so hard that Dan thought she might break a rib.

"Nora?"

"Screw you, Dan. The last thing in the world I want to be doing is looking for a new husband. A new lover. A new anyone. But you got so gobbled up in that creative head of yours that you lost sight of the deal."

"What deal?"

"The wedding deal, you asshole. The one where you love me and cherish me and lie to me when I get passed over for a promotion, and tell me I'm amazing. The one where you swear to adore me in sickness and in health, and pull your head out of your sanctimonious ass long enough to notice that your wife went back on the Pill three months ago because she lost hope that you cared enough to even try to have a baby with her." Her eyes flashed with fury. "Do you remember that contract we signed in City Hall? It was right there in the fine print. I, Dan Peterson, swear to never mention my loving wife's new gray hairs. I promise to rub her feet when her shoes are killing her and bring her chamomile tea when her cramps are bad, and ignore the fact that she's in spitting distance of menopause and scared half to death of having to start all over again."

Dan's jaw hung open like a busted gate. Out of the corner of his eye he noticed Nora's screen. The sexy logo of CNN flashed uselessly behind her. Perhaps he had miscalculated when he first walked in the door.

"Nora?"

"What?"

"Did you sleep with him?"

"Jesus. I never even met him."

"You didn't?"

"No," she said with utter exasperation. "You are such a fool. Why would I need to go outside for that when I'm married to the poster child for Cialis? *If your erection lasts longer than four hours."*

Something that resembled a smile crossed Dan's face. He came towards her.

"Stop right there, Mister!"

"What?" he said, alarmed.

"You keep that thing in its holster. That is not what this is about."

He halted in his tracks. "Okay. I'm listening."

"You never listen."

"I love you."

"You love the idea of me."

"So what's wrong with that?"

"Goddammit Dan, I'm a person, not a character description. You can't just rewrite me to fit your needs. This is not a dress rehearsal."

"I know. Believe me, I know." He drooped all of a sudden, going all hangdog on her. She stared at him.

"You do?" Now it was Nora's turn to be surprised.

"Of course I do. You don't think I live in terror of that every single day?"

"In terror of what?"

"That you're right. This is it. My life. One long miserable dress rehearsal. With no curtain call in sight."

"But you're doing what you want," she said, throwing her hands up in helpless frustration. "You quit your day job for this."

"I quit my day job so I wouldn't rot on the vine before I ever had a chance for one lousy dream of mine to come true."

"But this is your dream."

"No, actually it's not. It's my worst nightmare."

She sighed. *Artists.* Did it ever get any easier?

"I am so sick and tired of this freaking one-act, I want to shred it like confetti and chuck it out the window."

Was that a tear she saw in the corner of his eye? There wasn't even an acting coach anywhere in sight. She had to hand it to him. He made an excellent Charlie Brown. *All I got was a rock.*

"Do you know what I pictured for you when I signed my new agent?" Dan said. Nora felt her guilt umbrella going up. "A two-bedroom with a river view on West End Avenue. With a study and a brand new iMac to write that novel of yours at last. I saw dinner parties that would put Lucy to shame, and a sweet little summer place way up the Taconic, and the doorman pooching our kid's hair in the stroller every time we headed out to the playground at 86th Street." He looked away.

"Oh Dan." She was starting to feel a little bit like the prize fool. "Sweetheart?" She put one hand tentatively on his wrist. A peace offering. His fingers curled around hers. "I'm sorry." And she meant it. She truly was.

He turned back towards her. "You're not leaving me for a doctor?" he asked in a raspy voice.

"Not even a specialist."

He allowed the smallest glimmer of a hopeful smile and inched closer on the couch. She noticed a familiar stirring in his gray bicycle shorts. Jeez, quick recovery, she thought. The guy had the attention span of a moth. Still, life could be worse. She kissed the salty sweat of his neck. Dan leaned back and closed his eyes. She peeled the dank t-shirt from his body. She could see her computer screen glowing behind him on the desk, its memory stripped of her brief liaison. The illicit phone number remained balled up in the back of the drawer. She ran her hands over Dan's chest. He groaned and started to reach for her, but she shoved him back down. This scene was from her script. One way or the other, she was going to take charge.

- 32 -
LUCY

The gentle chirp of the house phone startled her awake. She sprung up from the leather chair. Early morning light filtered through the study windows. Nothing good came of calls at this hour. She had not been to bed all night. She braced herself.

"Hello?" she said.

"It's me. She's okay."

Lucy felt the tears well up as she listened to Paula's voice, disconnected and distant, somewhere out in central New Jersey. She paced about the living room, registering bits of information – Missy and her friends were out drinking, partying, craziness ensued. There was vodka and marijuana; no one was driving, no one was seriously hurt.

Lucy heard her own soothing words spring from her lips, clichéd and rote. What did it matter what she said. Tragedy had been averted, a parent's bullet dodged. Paula and Chuck were spared. Funny, she didn't even think of Missy's health and well-being. The kids, they were resilient. But what sixteen-year-old could fathom the emotional damage they wrought on everyone else with their reckless, unpremeditated actions? Her crazy night would be a story, a smile to share with friends at school on Monday morning. She'd sleep it off and live to tell another day. She wondered how Chuck and Paula would move on. How did any of them?

"We'll talk later, honey," Lucy said. "Thank God she's all right. Give Chuck a big hug for me, okay?" She paused.

"Yes, we love you too."

She laid the phone back in its cradle and leaned against the windowsill. Her back was stiff and painful. She had dozed on and off, curled up like a cat in Lionel's chair. The first rays of daybreak were casting an orange glow across the burnished top of his piano. In the distance she could see the mist rising off the East River. No wonder he liked it here so much. The stillness of the study was serene, like a cathedral. The valise still sat packed on the floor. Funny, Lucy thought, fingering the worn fabric of the overnight bag. Had Lionel stumbled upon it only recently, or had it been fueling his jealousy for years?

She picked it up as if it were radioactive. No guessing what other unintended consequences it might set off. She walked out of the study, snatching up her stiletto heels where she had left them the night before. As she headed down the hall, it struck her. Lionel might be gone. The thought sent a shiver down her spine. She poked her head through the bedroom door. His unruly mop of hair filled the pillow. His chest rose and fell with sleep. She breathed an unexpected sigh of relief. He looked like a lion in repose, she thought. A wounded creature, no different than the rest of us.

She set the valise down on the bed and unsnapped the clasp locks. She pried the case open. She hadn't looked in it for years. How odd to finger the worn remnants from her past. Just caressing the frayed L.L. Bean flannel shirt took her back to a high school boyfriend whose hands had undone those very buttons. She smiled softly. At least Lionel didn't suspect that one. Beneath the clothes she found an old

Maybelline makeup kit. Her mother must have added that later. Only a woman married in 1954 would consider lipstick and blush the panacea to whatever ills a bad marriage might throw one's way.

Lucy lifted each item from the bag and laid it on the bed. In the space of a few seconds it was empty. She snapped it shut with a click. She looked up from her handiwork. Lionel was awake, gazing at her. The crow's feet around his eyes were deep and furrowed. He looked good in the morning light, she decided. Handsome and mature, like a man you'd want to have around.

"You're still here," he said.

"I was thinking the same about you."

She picked up one piece of clothing at a time and set it deliberately in her dresser drawer. No matter that it was her youth she was packing away. Everything had its rightful place. Lionel watched in silence until she had buried every last bit of evidence.

"The phone rang before," Lionel said.

"She's okay."

"Thank God."

"Yes. Thank God." Lucy sat down at the edge of the bed. She was still in her black cocktail dress. It had been a long night. The luster of the fabric had faded. She wriggled out of the dress, slipped off her panties, and pulled herself under the thick white comforter, nude, careful not to touch Lionel as she lay her head down on her pillow. She stared up at the ceiling.

Lionel peered at her, a bemused look of childlike curiosity on his face. "I love you, you know," he said.

"You do?"

"More than anything."

"Why?"

"Why?" he asked in a surprised voice.

"Yes, why. I've done nothing. I don't deserve you."

"You make an exquisite tuna tartare."

"What?" Lucy cocked her head sideways at him like a sparrow.

"The way you chop the fish into perfect little eighths. Never a piece off. And then you add the oil and lemon and cilantro and black pepper. I love the way you knead it all together, probing it with your fingers, popping those fleshy little bits into your mouth for a sample taste. And when you have it just right – you know how can I tell?" She shook her head, wondering if her husband had lost his mind. "You have this habit. You clap your hands together like Charlie Chaplin. Whenever I hear that muffled *pouf pouf pouf*, I know you've created something amazing. Something so good and so real. And I envy you more than you can ever know. It inspires me. It reminds me of the way you picked me out on that concert hall stage, not a chance in the world you weren't going to get precisely what you wanted."

Lucy turned away. "I was supposed to be more."

"More what?"

"More successful. More engaged. More able to change the world. More, everything."

"You were to me."

"Is that enough?"

"You gave us a child."

She looked back at him and nodded. "True. As specimens go, I suppose I'm a good example of flesh and blood biology – a uterus that delivered a product we loved and nurtured. I'll give you that."

"You know you're more, Luce. Everything you do, you do well. Your committees. Your volunteer work. The way you raised our son."

"Don't patronize me. You make me sound so pedestrian. So Westchester circa 1963. I should be wearing a goddamned Betty Crocker apron or a pillbox hat."

"Lucy," he scowled. How had they arrived here? What had begun as a friendly evening amongst friends had devolved into the hunting scene from *La Regle de Jeu*. They had all become ensnared in traps of their own devising.

"You could do better than me, Lionel."

"I don't want to."

"I've let you down."

"How?"

"I lied. There *is* someone else."

She watched the air sail out of him like a gigantic punctured balloon. And in that yawing sinkhole of a moment – the time between the truth he needed to know and the one he was fabricating in his mind – she realized she had been wrong. Wrong for hiding her unhappiness for so long, and wrong for not letting him in. For what good was marriage without trust? Beyond the courtship and the honeymoon and all the flirting and fucking and fluids in between – the petty jealousies and imagined betrayals, the babies and the mortgage and the whole goddamned disaster – what possible reason was there for humans to engage in such frivolous behavior? There could only be one answer. To come clean and be un-judged. To squeeze yourself out like a giant tube of protoplasm and pain and hurt and say: *Take me as I am.*

Lionel stared at her from across the chasm of their king-sized bed. He had never pretended to be anything but who he was. Raw, honest, vulnerable. He had tumbled over the precipice with her. Why had she not done the same?

She sat up cross-legged. She had given up a part of herself long ago, and now she wanted it back. Even if it meant risking she was going to lose another. She reached across the space between them and stroked Lionel's craggy, unshaven cheek. He did not flinch.

"Li," she said with every last ounce of honesty she could muster. "There's something I have to tell you."

His expression held such unspeakable intensity – the tortured machinations of a grown man intermingled with the longing of a little boy – that she smiled. She couldn't help herself.

"What are you laughing about?" he asked. "What could possibly be funny at a moment like this?"

"Well, Lionel," she said. "Here's the thing. The other man? He's not a man. He's a boy."

Lionel looked at her like she'd just sprouted wings.

"*My* boy. I have a son. From long ago."

She watched as he drank in her words. His eyebrows furrowed so sharply she thought they might draw blood.

"I don't understand," he said. "I've known you since, well——. It's not possible. Is it?"

"It is. Something happened. In another life. When I was a student."

"At Brown?"

"No. It was on my semester abroad." *In London of all places, she thought with delicious irony.*

"But how? How could you keep it a secret?" She could see him fumbling with this newfound information like a slippery bar of soap.

"I've never told anyone. I didn't even know myself." She realized how preposterous that sounded. "I mean I knew I had a baby. I was nineteen. I'd gone over to England for school early. To get set up and all? And I was lonely. I didn't know anyone. I met a jazz player. In a nightclub."

Lionel groaned.

"Yes, dear, I'm sorry. A musician. Even back then. It

was a one-night stand." She shrugged. It was a little late to call out the morality police.

"A one night stand? And you got pregnant?" He contemplated this, the trickle of details starting to catch up with his previous sense of impending doom. "Bloody unlucky."

"Tell me about it."

"So why didn't you—?" His voice trailed off at the mention of the obvious.

"Have an abortion? I was going to. That's what liberal Jewish girls did back then. It was all the craze. I had a clinic lined up. I was on the calendar. But something stopped me. I just couldn't."

"Why?"

"I don't know," she said softly. "I wanted to be – different?" A whole new expression was painting Lionel's face. She wondered if it was concern or relief. "So I decided to go through with the pregnancy and give up the child for adoption."

"That's quite the semester abroad program."

"No kidding."

"But how did you manage? Pregnant and alone and taking classes?" He puzzled for a moment. "And you said it was a semester. That's not nine months."

"I stayed an extra term. My parents thought I'd landed an internship at the House of Commons. They were thrilled for me. They wanted to come and visit. That took a village to stop them."

"I bet."

"Even Dan and Nicole didn't know. I didn't tell a soul. My little secret."

"I don't know how you did it."

"I don't either. It wasn't easy, believe me. But there was

no email of course, so no one was tracking my movements every second. You needed a grocery bag full of shillings to make one phone call to the States from the pay phone in the hall. Privacy was just an easier affair. All it took was a packet of stationery and a sheaf of international stamps to keep the world at bay. And I did. I wrote letters until my wrists cramped. Every last one of them a lie."

Lionel propped himself up on one elbow, chin in hand. The pieces were all coming together.

"He was born on April 5th," Lucy continued. "I was on a plane home three weeks later."

"Wow." It was a word her husband rarely used. "The adoption went quickly."

"It was all pre-arranged."

"You were organized. Even back then."

Lucy nodded. It was not exactly the adjective she would have come up with, but then again, it had been so long ago. There were a lot of blanks she had never bothered to fill in. She was new at this.

"So who were the adoptive parents?"

"I never met them. The hospital takes the baby as soon as it's born. Otherwise, what mother would ever give up her child?" Lucy felt the chill from the open window on her naked shoulders. She pulled the comforter up for cover.

Lionel breathed in deeply, then exhaled like he was struggling to evict something. "So why now, Lucy? Why did you go looking for him after so many years?"

"Oh my God, no. I didn't. That's not what happened at all. A letter came. Six months ago. From an agency here in New York. The kind that links up adopted children searching for their birth parents."

Lionel pondered this. "So that's where you were going on the subway," he said at last. "You visit him."

"He lives in an apartment in Harlem," Lucy replied. She could see her reflection in the mirror by the door. Her mascara from the night before had run. She looked like she had two black eyes.

"You have a son," Lionel announced suddenly, as if he'd just discovered the Higgs boson.

"Yes. Two sons."

For a man who made his living composing intricate lines of interweaving music, Lucy could see that tidy little factoid taking its time to sink in.

"How old is he?"

"He'd be twenty-four now."

"You've never met him?"

"No. I sit on a park bench across the street from his apartment building and I watch. From afar."

"I see." Lionel deflected his gaze out the window, as if he were searching for something.

"Why didn't you tell me, Lucy?" he said at last.

"I didn't know how to. The letter came as such a shock."

"Not now. Then. When we first met."

Lucy sighed. "I'm not sure. Maybe I was ashamed? Maybe it was a truth best left buried? I don't know. I guess I'd hoped to be a better person. Not the kind of woman who abandons her child."

She turned away. She'd had enough. She got out of bed and started to rummage for some clothes to throw on. Lionel watched her. She moved as casually as if she were heading to the market.

"Where are you going?" he asked.

"You probably want some time," she replied.

"For what?"

"To decide what you want to do?"

"It's eight in the morning. What might I want to do?"

"I don't know. Leave me?"

He cast her a curious glance, like she'd asked him to take out the garbage. Or prepare a soufflé from scratch. "And why would I want to leave you?"

"Because I had a child out of wedlock. That I gave away like a houseplant. And I've been lying to you. For twenty-four years." She felt the tears welling up. Lionel reached out with one hand, beckoning her back to bed. She came and sat down on the edge.

"What do you want, Lucy?"

She paused. It was so obvious. Why not just blurt it out. "I want to meet my son." There. She said it. Funny. After so many years, and then all those months of sitting in guilty silence on a Harlem park bench, she finally realized with complete unwavering certainty – it was time.

"That's it?"

"I guess so." She gave a small shrug, a slip of a gesture – an understatement of epic proportions. She was not quite on to next steps yet. "What do *you* want, Lionel?"

"You," he replied without hesitation.

"Really?" she said.

"It's all I've ever wanted. The rest is baggage."

She looked at him with the hint of a grin. "You mean like a dusty old valise?"

"Precisely. Something we can toss back in the closet and completely forget about." He traced his finger along the smooth skin of her wrist. The rosy hue of dawn had been replaced by growing sunlight. Sunday morning, he mused. Bagels, lox. *The New York Times*. Another day.

A cloud crossed Lucy's face.

"What is it?" Lionel asked.

"What if he wants to come live with us?"

"Oh Luce. Don't you think we should take this one step

at a time?"

"Okay." She hopped up and crawled back to her side of the king-sized bed. Lionel lifted the comforter in a huge billowing cloud and swept her underneath. They lay apart like that for a while, not speaking. Lionel cleared his throat.

"Lucy?"

"Lionel?"

"I was right, you know."

"About what?"

"You had sex with another man."

"Yes, my love. But only one. And only once."

Lucy smiled to herself, because she was right, too. She slid across the acres of 400-count Ralph Lauren cotton until she was close to Lionel, the two of them staring up at the ceiling, sharing the pillow. There was nothing left to hide. So she closed her eyes. And at last, sleep came.

- 33 -
CODA

Cool autumn air covered the city like a blanket. Puffy clouds hung like cotton candy over an arch blue sky. An errant newspaper page skittered across the sidewalk in the brisk northerly breeze. It clung to Lucy's ankle until she shook it off.

"Perhaps we should go ring?" Lionel suggested.

Lucy nodded, resting with one arm laced through his. She was in no hurry. They sat on the park bench like an elderly couple. All we need is our walkers and a flock of pigeons by our feet, she thought. Lionel's overcoat smelled nice, like cigar smoke and cologne. She could stay here forever if need be.

"What if he's not home?"

"It's Sunday afternoon, Lucy. People tend to be in at this hour."

She was out of excuses. They rose from the bench and walked across Madison Avenue. She could see nearly to midtown the street was so deserted. They let themselves into the lobby and stood in front of the ancient intercom system. The black, dot-sized button stared out at her. There was no name, only the apartment number beside an empty slot for a tag. 4-E.

"Do you think this is a good idea?" she asked, her voice trailing off to a whisper.

"I do," replied Lionel. "Go ahead, love."

She depressed the button. A muted, tinny buzz emitted from the panel. She waited about two seconds. "He's not there."

"Lucy?"

"Okay." She pressed it one more time. A moment passed. She was already turning away when the speaker crackled to life.

"'ullo?"

An electric jolt ran through her. The familiar catch of the Cockney accent was unmistakable. As if it were a hot night in a London pub, twenty-four years gone by.

A pause. Then the voice crackled again. "Allo then. Who is it?"

Lucy stared at the mesh screen of the intercom, and then at Lionel. He nodded. She took a deep breath and leaned up close, putting her mouth to the speaker. It was time to answer that question.

ACKNOWLEDGMENTS

My heartfelt thanks to everyone who contributed to The Dinner Party. Without you, *Food for Marriage* would not have happened.

Victoria Skurnick plucked this novel from the unsung galaxy of hungry authors and breathed professional life into it. Toby Elrod sparked the notion that there was a new way to make a book. Howie, Joy, Susie and Ralph looked over my shoulder with wise, unblurred eyes. Ted Baer has been there for every last word in the name of art. Linda Loewenthal is an inspiration to anyone who writes. And a year of breakfasts in Greenwich Village with Chef John DeLucie was my template for every recipe that worked, both for Lucy and for me.

John Heins taught me all about good design and created a story in a cover before there was even a title. And the Boulder gang has supported the whole creative enterprise since draft one.

In the early influence department, all due to Blossom, who put the raw egg in the chopped meat and always let me taste. And Richard, who installed a 16mm movie projector behind the Marimekko in our basement, and first revealed to me that storytelling is a passion, not a job.

Fred, John, Steve, Mitch, Cali, Barb and Jeanne: I owe you a lot of drinks. Your encouragement has been unwavering.

Sean and Emilia, you made Wilmette a test kitchen, a writer's den, and my second home.

Ben and Matty, every last word is for The KMB Club. Always.

And Geri, who never takes no for an answer. Thank you for teaching me yes.

ABOUT THE AUTHOR

KEN CARLTON is the author of four previous nonfiction works, including *The Hunger*, which he co-wrote with Manhattan chef John DeLucie. *The Hunger* was a Barnes & Noble Discover Great New Writers selection and was included in *Best Foodwriting of 2009*. Carlton is a graduate of Middlebury College and The American Film Institute. He and his wife, a professor, commute between their two homes, four children, and two dogs in Brooklyn and Chicago. *Food for Marriage* is his first novel.

www.kencarlton.net

Made in the USA
Lexington, KY
29 April 2014